Terror by Design

Other Avalon Books by Jane Edwards

THE HESITANT HEART
THE GHOST OF CASTLE KILGARROM
SUSANNAH IS MISSING!

TERROR BY DESIGN

Jane Edwards

AVALON BOOKS
THOMAS BOUREGY AND COMPANY, INC.
401 LAFAYETTE STREET
NEW YORK, NEW YORK 10003

Library of Congress Catalog Card Number: 89-81639
ISBN 0-8034-8793-2

PRINTED IN THE UNITED STATES OF AMERICA
BY HADDON CRAFTSMEN, SCRANTON, PENNSYLVANIA

This book is for Jeanne Rogers
To celebrate a friendship that began long, long ago at the Villa Maria Academy in Frontenac, Minnesota

Jane Campbell Edwards

Chapter One

The computer was down . . . again.

Scooting her chair back from the workstation feeding into the lab's state-of-the-art equipment, Rae Travis kept a tight rein on her temper. Though there were times when she was tempted to suspect that this particular piece of high-tech wizardry had it in for her personally, she knew that the opinion of the maintenance crew tended to slant in the opposite direction. So far as they were concerned, she was one technical systems developer who should stick to a drafting table and graph paper.

Deep in her heart Rae was beginning to wonder if they might not be right. To the point where, for the past several weeks, the most intricate and innovative of her designs for Project G.A.T.E. had been painstakingly drawn by hand, rather than being worked out with the assistance—or otherwise—of that temperamental electronic monster.

Sooner or later, though, the entire program would need to be entered into the central system. It was essential, Rae knew, to make certain that the shields she had so painstakingly developed—the entire protective-device apparatus that she always thought of as her "guardian angel package"—meshed with the exciting new avionics systems being formulated by the other members of the team.

No doubt, she thought with a touch of gloom, that would be the day every chip, every color-coded wire, every millimeter of microcircuitry in the entire computer system would decide to shut down altogether.

She really should get a dart board up here, Rae chided herself, and work off the worst of her aggressions on it rather than sniping at a blameless machine. Waiting a few moments until her natural good humor had been at least partially restored, she called down to Maintenance, asking that a technician be dispatched to her office.

"Same old problem?"

"Seems to be," Rae advised the unenthusiastic-sounding organizer she was speaking with. "The keyboard's stuck. The only response I get from it is a drone."

"It shouldn't be doing that," he grumbled, implying that it *wouldn't* be doing that if somehow or other she hadn't managed to mistreat the delicate circuits. She'd be there, wouldn't she, to furnish the key symbols the repairperson would need to delve into the depths of the system that held so many secrets?

"Where would I go?" Rae asked reasonably. "There's work to be done, worse luck. The longer I sit here talking, the further behind my schedule becomes. Please do your best to get him up here immediately."

Her fingers tightened over the receiver. She was tempted to reiterate that word "him," or at least specify that they dispatch anyone except Alyssa Fairfax to tend to the problem. But she couldn't quite bring herself to give in to her baser instincts and imply that Alyssa's work wasn't up to par simply because the darned girl rubbed her the wrong way.

In all honesty, Alyssa was probably the most skillful technician the lab possessed, Rae admitted. She had a hunch that the reason they didn't get along was due to a culture clash, pure and simple. She didn't know exactly where the other woman was from—they'd never gotten that friendly. Wherever it was, they didn't stress politeness there.

Rae herself was a Southerner, trained since birth in small pleasantries, natural courtesies, and a soft, gentle way of speaking. She didn't believe that being considerate of the feelings of others made any person, man or woman, less competent professionally.

Three years ago she had graduated in the top five percent of her class at the University of Miami. Since then she'd earned a master's in technical design, focusing on reinforcing and upgrading safety features aboard jet planes. She had also undergone a period of rigorous training before proving herself worthy of her present specialized job. For the past fourteen months she had served as a government employee. With others here at the lab, she was engaged in a highly classified project to protect her nation's aircraft.

Rae gathered up several sheets of paper containing notes and technical diagrams. Enclosing them in a folder, she locked them away in the voice-access wall safe. All data relating to Project G.A.T.E. was kept there when it wasn't in active use. No matter which of the maintenance people was sent to work on the computer, such material was not for their eyes. Their security clearances were good . . . but not that good.

Mulling over her antipathy to Alyssa Fairfax, she decided it was the woman's caustic comments about everyone from the director's secretary, Dana Webb, to Rae's own immediate superior, Dr. Cole Hamilton, that made Rae prefer to steer clear of her. Of course, it didn't exactly help matters that Alyssa had a thoroughly annoying way of acting as if Rae did something deliberately to cause the high-tech equipment at her workstation to break down.

"You catch more flies with honey," Rae's grandmother always used to caution. Alyssa's sharp-tongued complaints and intolerant attitude toward other people's minor shortcomings was the furthest thing from sweet Rae could imagine.

But maybe, she decided with a laugh, Alyssa simply didn't like flies!

Rae's comments to the maintenance dispatcher had included one bit of truth stretching. Rather than being behind schedule in her work, she was actually well ahead of her projected goal. Nevertheless, she found it exasperating to stop in the middle of an important task because of a mechanical breakdown. The quicker they could get that computer fixed, the more pleased she would be.

Meanwhile there was nothing to do but wait.

Indulging in a luxurious stretch, she strolled over to the window. She opened the window and leaned out. The afternoon was fiercely hot, unusually so even for July on the lower west coast of Florida. Below, one of the sentries, attracted by the flash of sunlight on her short, coppery hair, broke stride and sent her a friendly salute.

She waved back, smiling in sympathy at his woebegone appearance. The usually starchy marine looked decidedly wilted. A repetition of today's record temperature would probably blister the paint right off the signs.

Wired to the ten-foot fence that the Marines patrolled day and night, the signs were so blatant that not even a myopic bat could have failed to notice them. From her vantage point at the window, Rae easily made out the boldly slanting letters that proclaimed:

U.S. GOVERNMENT PROPERTY

UNAUTHORIZED PERSONNEL KEEP OUT!

The second sign was too near the gate and pointed the wrong way to be readable from the inner side of that tall fence, but Rae faced it every morning while waiting in line to present her ID pass for the guards' careful scrutiny: *SHELL BAY AVIONICS LABORATORY*

Beyond the fence stretched the town, bustling even in the heat and twice as large as it had been three years ago. Shell Bay was no longer typical of so many of the Gulf Coast towns hovering just above the Everglades—lethargic and stagnant, depending on orange groves and winter tourists from the North for their economy. Since the completion of the Avionics Laboratory it had become a full-grown city. Hundreds of new, upscale, permanent residences now shared the tax base with the wide-spaced and comfortable island-style homes scattered along the sandy, shell-littered beaches.

A no-nonsense knock brought Rae's thoughts sharply back to the present. Hastily she jerked her head back inside and closed the window before hurrying across the compact space to the door. The floor had been fully carpeted, the walls and ceilings acoustically tiled to keep "white noise" to a minimum. She was well aware that these particular materials also made it easy to identify "bugs." Frequent electronic sweeps were made for listening and monitoring devices that, in spite of the rigid security precautions enforced at the lab, might find their way onto the premises.

So far as Rae was aware, none had shown up since she'd been an employee here. She was all for keeping the status quo.

As she swung open the door to the corridor, she stifled a sigh. Her subtle hint to Maintenance hadn't worked. "Hello, Alyssa. Thanks for being so prompt," she greeted the other woman, who might have been two or three years older than she. Turning, she led the way over to the workstation and explained that she had no more than activated the equipment when it started to balk.

"Is it possible there's some sort of glitch down in its inner works?" Rae asked. "Honestly, I can't think of any other reason why it should break down with such regularity."

A glint in the attractive, dark-haired technician's eyes hinted that malfunctions didn't just happen—not when people knew how to handle sensitive instrumentation. But if that was what she was thinking, she did manage to hold her tongue for a change.

"Anything's possible," Alyssa admitted. She scowled down at the keyboard. "If these problems continue to arise, I may recommend that this unit be pulled out of service. At least until a thorough check can be run on the microcircuitry."

Wonders, Rae thought, would never cease. Was this their Alyssa, actually making an effort to be congenial? Then as she watched the other woman open the toolbox of streamlined instruments she carried, her conscience gave her a jab. How did she know what sort of problems Alyssa had to cope with? This piece of equipment might often provide the last straw after a day of mounting aggravations.

Without waiting to be asked, Rae provided that afternoon's key entry code and her personal access authorization, which would allow Alyssa to delve into the computer's delicate innards. Both sets of symbols changed twice daily on a random permutation of number groups impossible either to predict or to duplicate.

Except with that code in hand, the President himself couldn't have approached that computer without setting off a series of alarms guaranteed to place the state's entire southwest coast on red alert.

Alyssa was still bent diligently over the keyboard when, following a perfunctory knock, Dr. Hamilton swung into the room, his long white lab coat flapping behind him.

"Rae, I think I've ironed out that vapor-lock problem at last!" His exuberant announcement broke off instantly when he became aware that another person was in the room.

How difficult it must be for him, Rae thought, to constantly guard his tongue after almost three decades of working in the much more liberal atmosphere of a university teaching/research position. In the past Cole Hamilton's experiments had been carried out in the company of an eager group of undergraduates. His students participated in the trial-and-error efforts, then analyzed the results in written reports and endless classroom discussions.

Here in the Avionics Lab, on the other hand, he was allowed to mention his vitally important work only to the handful of colleagues who shared responsibility for completing their current task. Project G.A.T.E. was strictly a need-to-know operation.

"You mean the vapor lock that's been affecting the refrigerator in your motor home?" Tactfully Rae steered the conversation onto the first safe subject she could think of. She felt sure that if Alyssa did overhear an indiscreet remark and could manage to make sense of it, she would be horrified at the notion that she might be in possession of information affecting the security of the nation's airlines. But even an innocent comment outside these walls might be overheard by the wrong person and give their adversaries a vital clue as to what was going on here.

Fortunately Alyssa appeared not the least bit interested in the exchange between the skilled design team. Her level black brows puckered in concentration as she twirled a tiny steel rod between capable fingers. Its pointed tip made microscopic adjustments to a swirling coil of multicolored wires deep inside the computer. Though these were no thicker than strands of thread, Rae was well aware that running through the slender filaments were enough energy impulses to vector a giant transport plane on a globe-circling journey.

"Yes. Yes, the refrigerator." Cole Hamilton ran an agitated hand through thinning, sandy-gray hair and gratefully proceeded to build on Rae's helpful hint. "I've been thinking about driving down to the Keys some weekend soon and taking that fishing trip I keep promising myself. The outing will be much more enjoyable if I'm able to keep my supplies chilled en route."

"I should say so. Especially in this weather," Rae backed him up.

Her smile applauded his quick shift of gears. She

was very fond of her superior and sadly aware of the minimal amount of pleasure his life contained since the tragic death of his wife and two sons. Someday soon she was going to see to it that he *did* take that trip down to the Keys. The chain of small islands connected by the Overseas Highway extended for more than two hundred miles into the Gulf of Mexico, curving in a graceful arc between Miami and Key West.

Meanwhile she was making plans to see that at least one of his longtime dreams came true.

The reliable topics of weather and travel saw them through the next quarter hour while Alyssa completed her painstaking chore. She closed up the computer once again, then demonstrated that the circuits were in perfect condition.

Rae took a seat at the workstation. She ran off a few lines on the keyboard to assure herself that the electronic marvel was willing to cooperate with her own touch. The back-tilted screen faithfully reproduced every thought and symbol as her fingers moved along.

"Seems to be just fine." She looked up, smiling her thanks for the other woman's competent input. "Let's hope there'll be no need for you to come tinker with this creature anytime soon again."

Alyssa's faint smile indicated that she'd believe that when she saw it. "Let's hope," she repeated and closed the toolbox with an efficient snap.

* * *

Dana Webb was engrossed in her routine end-of-the-day disposal procedures when Rae entered Dr. Rausch's office two hours later. As the lab director's executive secretary, Dana had a great deal of sensitive material pass through her hands. She made quite sure nothing ever went any further without authorization.

Though Rae herself had grown increasingly security conscious since becoming involved with Project G.A.T.E., she never failed to be awed by the elaborate care Dana took to avoid leaving so much as a gum wrapper in her wastebasket. Pages from her shorthand books, scratchpad jottings from her boss's desk, and even the pink "while you were out" telephone-message forms joined research notes and the film ribbons from her electronic typewriter in the shredder. The spaghettilike residue was then transferred to a compact office incinerator. With one low whirr, the refuse was cremated into a sooty pile of ashes.

"I've been thinking of investing in a new garbage-disposal unit to replace that growling potato-peel eater in our sink." Rae's remark was only half teasing. "You don't suppose—"

"You know as well as I do that your dad would short-circuit the whole town, trying to dispose of bent fish hooks, if you bought one of these!" In that regard Dana had no illusions about her future father-in-law.

"Sad to say, you're absolutely right." Rae gave an exaggerated sigh of anticipation as she wiggled her toes in their leather shoes. "Thank heaven it's Friday. I don't intend to wear anything on my feet except toenail polish the next couple of days. How about you? Any ambitious plans for the weekend?"

"I wish! Brian's been attempting to wangle a three-day pass. Since he hasn't phoned, I'm assuming that it didn't materialize." Dana looked regretful but resigned. The Coast Guard had plenty of restrictions where the free time of its junior officers was concerned. She and Rae's brother, Brian, had announced their engagement two months earlier, but were postponing their wedding plans until he had completed his military service.

"My folks are planning a trip out to Sanibel. I might as well tag along," Dana decided. "Why don't you come too?"

Rae shook her head, thinking of the sweltering sixty-mile trip up Highway 41 and the droves of weekend shellers sure to be elbowing each other out of the way for a clear spot on one of the barrier island's famous beaches. "Not this time, thanks. Jeff is going to take me to see the brand-new Indiana Jones movie at the complex tonight. Since I have a favor I want to ask him, it probably wouldn't be a good idea to stand him up."

Tossing a "See you Monday" over her shoulder, Rae headed down to the building's main floor. There she joined the straggling line of employees waiting at the exit. Most of the lab's personnel had already departed for the weekend. There was only a brief wait before she, too, was passed through the sentry-controlled X-ray eye, a precaution against people who might be tempted to take their work home with them. Heading for the parking lot, she welcomed the soft breeze ruffling her hair. Anything less than a hurricane would have been appreciated today.

Three miles later she turned off the highway onto the crushed-shell road that snaked down to the beach. Her thoughts dwelled with satisfaction on the solution Dr. Hamilton had proposed to the vapor-lock problem he had been struggling to surmount for the past week or so. It seemed as if that were another design dilemma the avionics team had managed to over—

BANG!

The sharp echo of the blow-out was still resounding in Rae's ears when the steering wheel jerked, flinging her to the right. The shoulder harness dragged her back. Thankful for its rigid protection, she wrenched at the wheel and overcorrected, unnerved by the sudden loss of control over her usually reliable Ford. Her hands felt slick with perspiration. Holding on for dear life, she fought the urge to stamp on the brakes.

The blown rear tire sent the car careening giddily down the incline. A terrified glance took in gnarled mangrove trees lining both sides of the road. There was little she could do except attempt to decelerate the runaway engine gradually—and pray that no one got in her way.

Rae clamped a hand around the horn ring, sending up a raucous blare that startled a flock of brown pelicans into clumsy flight. Short, cautious jabs at the brake decreased her speed somewhat without upsetting the car's equilibrium. Desperately Rae tore the key from the ignition, but momentum propelled her onward.

Whipping around a curve, she faced the dead end of the Travis driveway. Either the house or the garage would flatten her car into scrap metal if she couldn't succeed in halting its violent thrust.

"Easy. Easy!" Rae breathed the warning with each swift stab at the brake. The driveway between the two buildings should be wide enough to take her through to the soft, sandy beach, where her tires would inevitably bog down. That's what she had to aim for. It was her only chance to finish this wild ride without damage or injury.

Ten yards from the driveway she risked another scared look at the scene ahead. For the first time she caught sight of the strange car looming just to the right of the garage. Directly in her path!

Rae crashed both feet against the brake pedal. The car bucked. Tires screeched. She pumped, floorboarded the brake again.

"Almost," she gasped. "Al—"

A bruising impact jolted her back in the seat. The motor roar sputtered to a cough, then abruptly died.

Fearfully Rae opened her eyes. She had come to a stop at last and appeared to be still alive, but the rear portion of the strange vehicle was no longer a smooth, green curve.

For a moment the caved-in trunk was all she managed to take in. Seconds later, though, she was gulping in horror as the significance of the whiplashed antennas and the distinctive spotlight atop the other automobile's roof dawned on her.

"Oh, no!" Rae groaned. "I've hit a police car!"

Chapter Two

Running footsteps tattooed across the ground. Numb with shock, Rae could only blink dazedly when her father jerked open the car door.

"Are you all right? You're not hurt?" he demanded anxiously.

"I—I'm fine, Dad. Thanks to the seat belt, I seem to be all in one piece." She climbed out stiffly, unable to drag her apprehensive gaze from the damage her precipitate entry had caused. "But, that poor car! Whose is it?"

"Mine, I'm afraid."

Rae wheeled around, focusing on the source of the mournful voice. She saw a tall, lean man with dark hair and a rugged jaw. Crinkles fanned out from the sides of his brown eyes, but there was no telling if the lines had been caused by squinting or smiling. He certainly wasn't smiling now.

Her rueful gaze dropped to the gold eagle insignia pinned to his uniform pocket. Law and order, all right—but not one of the more familiar branches.

Once again she glanced around at the official spotlight.

Dan Travis intercepted the questioning look. "Honey, meet Simon Kirk, a new border patrolman just assigned to this area. My daughter Rachel, inspector." His supporting arm tightened around her shoulders. "Come on; let's go inside. We can worry about the damage later, after you've told us what happened."

While Rae dropped down on the comfortable living-room divan, her father made a quick trip into the kitchen for the large, frosty pitcher of lemonade that was a summertime fixture in the Travis household. Returning, he filled tall glasses of the cooling beverage and handed them around to Rae and Simon Kirk, neither of whom had uttered a single word during his absence.

Rae's hands were still far from steady. The glass shook as she raised it to her lips and took a deep swallow.

"Listen," Simon Kirk said awkwardly, "just take a minute to relax, will you? You're going to choke if you chugalug that tart stuff down so fast."

She realized the truth of what he said. "Guess I was more shaken up than I realized," she admitted, lowering the glass onto the coffee table. "That was my first blow-out, and trying to handle it proved to be quite a battle."

"Those sharp pieces of shell can be treacherous." Dan Travis looked pretty shook-up himself. "How fast had you been driving?"

"No more than twenty-five or thirty, but the road drops steeply coming down to the beach. The car just seemed to keep gaining momentum, no matter what I did. I remember your warning me years ago never to jam on the brakes if something like that happened, so I did everything I could think of to slow it down gradually. It wasn't working, though. I figured my one chance was to aim for the driveway and try to shoot right through, where I'd bog down on the beach. Unfortunately—"

"Unfortunately, I'd left my car in the way," Simon concluded the tale for her.

"Yes. I'm sorry."

He was obviously sorry too—sorry that he'd ever set foot on the property, most likely, Rae thought. But before he could reply, her dad was congratulating her on keeping her head and handling the situation like a veteran.

Rae realized she was lucky indeed not to have been injured. Matters could have been much worse. What was done was done; all she could do now was assure their visitor that the damage to his vehicle would be fully covered by their insurance policy.

"Did you stop by on official business?" she asked, suddenly curious as to the reason for his call. "Or were you just testing the friendliness of the local inhabitants?"

There was an almost unnoticeable pause before Simon replied. "It would probably be fair to say my call involved a little of both," he answered judiciously. "Getting acquainted with residents along the shore can be especially helpful in my line of work. To be honest, the Border Patrol relies on ordinary people like yourselves to help them keep an eye on the coastline."

"What on earth for?" Rae asked. But a logical answer occurred to her before he had time to respond. "Oh—smugglers, of course. But doesn't the DEA handle that?"

"Though you'd never know it from the newspapers, other things get smuggled into the country besides drugs," he said in a wry tone. "Illegal aliens are another major thorn in our side." He added that compared to most other law-enforcement agencies, the Border Patrol was a small, vastly understaffed organization. A minimum force had been assigned to patrol the more than two thousand miles of shoreline in Florida alone. "Believe me, we need the assistance of all the extra eyes and ears we can recruit."

"Before you made your spectacular entrance, the inspector was asking if we had noticed any strange craft around these waters," Dan Travis mentioned.

All Rae could do was shake her head. "I haven't spotted anything unusual, but of course there are hundreds of boats around the Shell Bay area. Except for a few good-sized cabin cruisers, most of them are water-ski boats, or little skiffs and rowboats."

"Those aren't the type of craft I had in mind. Tell me about the cruisers."

Rae shrugged. "This isn't Palm Beach or Fort Lauderdale. An eighty-foot yacht would stand out like a neon sign on the church. The cruisers are working boats. Dad knows more about them than I."

Her father explained that as the owner of a bait-and-tackle shop on the wharf, he was well acquainted with the skippers of the larger vessels. "I'd say we had eighteen or twenty forty-footers berthed near here. The owners hire out to sport fishermen by the day or week."

"Newcomers, any of them?"

"Now, son, you know that in the South you're a newcomer if your great-granddaddy was born as far away as the next township. Take yourself, for example. At a guess I'd say you hailed from Dade County originally but that for some years you've been working in another part of the country where they walk and talk a little hastier."

The younger man's expression indicated that the guess was right on target. "You have a good ear for accents."

"I hear a lot of voices," Dan Travis said. "And no, in answer to your question, none of the charter-boat captains are brand-new to the area. I'd say the last of them dropped anchor around here gettin' on for two years ago." He fixed an inquiring look on the visitor. "Anyone in particular you're looking for? We might be of more help if we knew a few more specifics."

Simon's face closed into a polite mask. "Frankly, I'm not sure exactly what I hoped to find. The idea I've been pursuing is just that, so far—an idea."

Rae's interest sharpened. Working as she did in a

need-to-know environment, she recognized a polite runaround when she heard one. Something, she thought, was going on in their community. Whatever it was, this lawman had no intention of sharing the details with the residents of Shell Bay, although he'd had no hesitation in requesting their cooperation.

She intercepted the quick glance he shot at the waterproof watch strapped to his tanned wrist. Decisively she set down her glass and stood up, to lead the way back to the door. "We'd better have a look at your car. Friday night's a busy time for tow trucks, I've heard."

Fortunately the green sedan proved capable of taking the road under its own steam, although both it and Rae's light-blue compact would require some painstaking bodywork to restore their assembly-line appearance. A call to the Travises' insurance agent started the ball rolling on having their coverage activated. Work on the official car was given top priority. Within a few minutes an appointment had been made for it to be brought into Barker's Garage first thing Monday morning.

"They'll furnish a loaner for you to drive while the repairs are being made." Rae jotted down the address of the repair shop, then handed it to Simon. "It might be a good idea for you to tell us how to get hold of you, in case there are papers we both need to sign."

"Sure." He furnished her with a phone number, adding that for the time being he was staying with Norm Peters, an officer who had served in the area for a number of years. "He and his wife have a spare room in their home. I'll be bunking there until we see how things go."

From this, Rae surmised that Simon Kirk's assignment here was only temporary. He wasn't after smugglers or illegal aliens in general, she thought; his investigation had a very specific target. They'd been facing the water as they talked. Noticing the watchful way those brown eyes of his assessed the coastline, she decided that he must be very good at what he did.

Without warning, that gaze was pulled back and fastened on her. With the same grave intentness he'd fixed on the boat traffic out in the Gulf, he now appraised her oval face, the layered coppery hair, the clear green eyes challenging his with keen intelligence. A flicker of personal interest stirred.

"I don't get much time off," Simon said unexpectedly.

Rae blinked. Was he saying he'd like to see her again but couldn't work it into his busy schedule? If so, it was certainly a novel approach. A hasty retort hovered on the tip of her tongue; she was tempted to remark that his lack of leisure hours was his tough luck, not hers. In the nick of time she got the impulse under control, reminding herself that only that afternoon she'd been putting Alyssa Fairfax down for her sharp-tongued comments.

"Cheer up," she said instead. "There's always a chance Shell Bay will turn out to be more law-abiding than you anticipated."

He climbed into his damaged car, pulled forward a few feet, then expertly backed around, coming to a precise halt only inches from where she was standing.

"Somehow," he said, "I don't think that problem is going to arise."

Problem? Rae walked back into the house. In the kitchen, her dad had taken a platter of newly filleted fish out of the refrigerator and was rubbing them with slices of lemon before layering them into the broiler pan. What kind of lawman, she mulled as she set out the salad greens, would consider it a *problem* to have his beat turn out to be free of criminal activities?

Her pensive silence drew her dad's attention. "Still shaken up from the accident? Maybe you'd better call off that date with Jeff. Stay home and take it easy instead."

"What? Oh, thanks, Dad, but I'm just fine."

With determination Rae yanked her thoughts away from the dark-eyed man she had found to be such an attractive enigma. He was only here on special assignment, she reminded herself. Furthermore, whatever that assignment involved seemed to have a twenty-four-hour-a-day lock on his attention. He had practically told her straight out that he didn't have time for women.

Briskly she rubbed the mahogany bowl with a slivered clove of garlic, then began tearing lettuce into bite-sized chunks. Why, she wondered, had Simon Kirk bothered to say anything at all? Why not just get into his dented car and go?

* * *

In the Travis household, domestic chores were split down the middle. KP duties were her father's responsibility this week. As soon as dinner was over, Rae headed upstairs for a refreshing shower. Twenty minutes later she was zipping up a pale green sun-dress and tucking her bare toes into a summery pair of high-heeled sandals. The shampoo had brought out shining highlights in the copper halo of her hair. The warm tone was echoed by a sprinkling of freckles across her nose. By late in her teens, Rae had stopped trying for a tan, facing the fact that not even the fierce Florida sun was going to turn her any color but a painful blistered red. Not caring to encounter skin problems later in life, she was smart enough not to tempt fate.

Punctuality was one of her virtues. Jeff Carter had just arrived when she descended the stairs again. "Ummm, don't you look tasty," he commented. "Like a nice fresh slice of Key lime pie."

"No wonder your growth got out of hand," Rae retorted with a laugh. "All you ever think about is food."

"Wanna bet?"

A wicked twinkle had appeared in Jeff's blue eyes. Rae felt a stab of irritation with herself for having given him such an obvious opening. They had been dating off and on for several months. At times she found it difficult to persuade Jeff to keep his hands to himself. But she did enjoy his company, and there was no denying that he was good-looking. Usually, as now, she found it best to pretend that his more outrageous banter went straight over her head.

The charter-boat captain was at least four inches over six feet, with a well-muscled physique gained in part from struggling to land powerful fighting gamefish that were even bigger than he was. His blond hair, bleached nearly platinum by the outdoor life he led, contrasted handsomely with his deeply tanned skin.

Rae felt a pang. What she wouldn't give for just a shade or two of that tan! "Honestly, Jeff," she pretended to grumble as she picked up her white purse and a lightweight sweater to toss around her shoulders in the frigidly air-conditioned theater, "I've seen tree bark paler than you are."

"Think so?" He seemed pleased. Who, his grin implied, wanted to be a paleface? "I like being out in the elements. Tell the truth, I'd probably stay aboard the *Coral Belle* full-time if it wasn't for the enticing attractions ashore."

Rae had already said good night to her dad. She was spared having to think of a tactful reply to Jeff's flattering comment by his exclamation of surprise when he stepped back out the door and for the first time caught sight of the damage to the Ford's left headlight. "What in tarnation did you hit?"

"Would you believe a police car?" She gave a self-conscious laugh. "Well—an official vehicle, anyway. It belonged to the new border patrolman in this neck of the woods. I had a blow-out coming down that slope from the main highway and wasn't able to get my car stopped in time."

"Oh, bad luck. They'll probably raise your insurance premium next time 'round," Jeff predicted blithely. "I didn't know we had a new inspector in the area. Norm Peters finally retire, did he?"

"Not that I know of. I guess they're going to be partners." *For a little while, anyway,* Rae added to herself. "He was here talking to Dad when I barreled into him. I gather his special focus is illegal aliens."

"You'd think the government would have more to worry about than a few harmless little foreigners who haven't had the good luck to make it in on their country's quotas," Jeff groused.

Somehow, Rae brooded uneasily, she didn't think the focus of Simon Kirk's investigation could be termed "harmless little foreigners." There'd been something in his watchful gaze, his guarded comments, that gave her the impression there was far more to his assignment than intercepting a few impoverished boat people.

She opened her lips to say so, then closed them again. Probably, like the work that went on in the Avionics Lab, the less said about that particular assignment, the better. Besides, what did it matter to her and Jeff?

The big-budget adventure movie proved to be an exciting treat. By the time the feature ended, Rae was feeling relaxed and cheerful once again.

"Jeff, that was a real winner," she thanked him.

"Being up to my neck in danger with Indiana Jones for the past two hours definitely made up for the whole rotten day."

"I had a heck of an experience myself this afternoon," he confided. "Some joker tried to charter my boat to catch salmon! I tried to tell him as tactfully as possible that he'd need to head over to the Pacific Coast for that particular pleasure, but I'm not sure he believed me."

Rae rolled her eyes and admitted that some people's expectations were pretty unrealistic. "Well, buck up—it's Friday."

"That might be consoling news for you, but I have charter parties booked for both tomorrow and Sunday." Jeff could hardly have looked less enthusiastic. "These are the kind of amateurs who will entangle themselves in the anchor chain and smear suntan lotion all over the decks, then blame me when we don't come up with a tarpon."

"Oh, that reminds me. I hope you aren't already booked up for Saturday after next. I want to charter the *Coral Belle* myself," Rae said. "It's Dr. Hamilton's birthday. Several times he's mentioned that he'd like to try fishing—"

Jeff let out a groan. "Another amateur!"

"True, but he's the only boss I've got, and he leads a pretty dull life."

"You couldn't just buy him a necktie instead? Or a ticket to the movies?"

"Why, Captain Carter, anyone would think you didn't *want* to charter your boat!" Anyone would also think he was just the teeniest bit jealous, Rae concluded. She stifled a sigh. A great many women would be delighted to find their time monopolized by the *Coral Belle*'s tall, good-looking skipper, but she had no intention of becoming serious about anyone.

For some peculiar reason Simon Kirk's lean, watchful face popped into her mind.

Not yet, anyway, she amended the previous thought.

Chapter Three

Bright and early the next morning Rae sat down to plan the menus for the following week's meals. Back in high school she had looked forward to living and working in a big city someday, with all the wonderful advantages such a setting had to offer. She had truly enjoyed her college years in Miami and brief vacations to such fascinating places as New Orleans and Savannah. But gradually Rae came to the conclusion that an urban life-style, with its crowds and noise and all-out competitiveness, wasn't for her. She was far happier in the smaller, more slow-paced milieu of Shell Bay.

The decision to return home had worked out well for the entire family. Her mother's health had never been exactly robust. By the time Rae had earned her master's degree and was ready for a full-time job, Marcella Travis was confined to bed most of each day. Rae had never been sorry that she'd made the decision to return to the friendly Gulf Coast community where she'd been born. Those last few months of quality time with her mom proved to be a very special period in her life.

After that, maintaining close family ties seemed to become more important than ever. Brian and she and their dad all had lives of their own to lead, of course, and separate interests. Still, the harmony they enjoyed as a family continued to deepen over the years.

How lucky for her, Rae thought now as she jotted items on her grocery list, that the Avionics Lab had opened nearby when it did. The government installation furnished her with a fulfilling, well-paid place to work while making it possible for her to stay close to the people she loved. Her technical-design specialty offered a highly creative and challenging career. She especially enjoyed the satisfaction of knowing that she was engaged in something important, even vital. Perhaps to the point of being able to prevent such tragedies as that which had claimed the lives of Dr. Hamilton's family from taking place in the future.

Rae had just finished scanning the weekend food-market ads when the crunch of tires on the driveway outside made her raise her head and push back her chair. The kitchen door burst open unceremoniously before she had a chance to see who had arrived. The next moment she was wrapped in a brotherly hug.

"Brian! Your pass came through, after all!" Rae stepped back, gazing up at the redheaded Coast Guardsman whose freckled features were a male version of her own. At twenty-three he was nearly three years younger than she, but somewhere along the line her "little" brother had outgrown her by half a foot. "Why didn't you phone and let us know you were on your way?"

"Wasn't time." Brian Travis tossed his white hat toward a chair. "At 0600 a drill we had planned was called off, so the exec decided to turn a few of us loose for seventy-two hours. Ten minutes later I was in a jeep headed for the airfield. I hitched a ride on one of our rescue helicopters as far as Fort Myers. The bus for Shell Bay was just pulling out of the terminal when I flagged it down. I'd have called you from the middle of town except, as luck would have it, the UPS driver hailed me. He was headed out this way with a package for the Brannigans—"

"So you came with him. Smart decision," Rae applauded his good judgment as she concluded the tale of his odyssey for him. "Sounds like you never had a minute to stop and eat."

"Well, I'd sure never turn down a couple of sandwiches and a quart of milk if someone was kind enough to offer them to me." Brian strode purposefully in the direction of the wall phone. "Want to fix 'em for me, Sis, while I give Dana a call?"

"Bad news, little brother. She won't be home." Rae opened the refrigerator and began setting out mustard and mayonnaise, cheese and lettuce, tomatoes, and a jar of sliced pickles. "She and her folks went up to Sanibel for the weekend. When you didn't call, we both figured that you'd be out on the cutter this week."

Disappointment replaced Brian's eager expression,

but he took the news of his fiancée's absence philosophically. "Oh, well. I'll catch her Sunday night. I don't have to start back until Monday." He found a bag of potato chips and ripped it open. "How's Dad doing?"

"Fine. Busier than a cat in a sardine factory. He's selling bait and tackle faster than he can take it out of stock. I suspect people are just anxious to get out on the water in this hot weather, whether the fish cooperate or not."

"I don't blame them. Must be ninety-five degrees out there already. At least the locals are content with snook or mullet. Northern visitors don't feel like they've had a good time unless they go home with an eight-foot-long tarpon to mount on their office wall."

His remark reminded Rae of Jeff Carter's disparaging comments about the amateur anglers who chartered the *Coral Belle.* The previous evening, after some persistence on her part, he had finally agreed to help her arrange the birthday surprise for Dr. Hamilton. Once he'd decided to be cooperative, he had even offered her the use of the cruiser at no charge—provided the lunch she brought aboard included plenty of fried chicken and Rocky Road ice cream.

"Well," she observed, trying to be fair, "without all those out-of-state vacationers, the economy along a big part of this coast would definitely be depressed. What have you been doing with your time? Had much patrol duty lately?"

A fleeting frown ruffled Brian's placid expression. It didn't match his response, the too-offhand statement that things were pretty much routine. It was a good thing her brother had opted to enlist for military service at sea, rather than aspiring to military intelligence, Rae decided. A poker face wasn't one of his assets.

Yesterday when Simon Kirk had sat in the living room telling them as little as possible about the purpose behind his questions, it had occurred to Rae that security considerations played a major role in both of their jobs. Now, for the first time, she found herself wondering whether Brian, too, occasionally encountered a situation during his duty hours that he wasn't allowed to talk about.

It still embarrassed her to remember that initial meeting with Simon Kirk. While her brother mowed down the plate of sandwiches she had fixed for him, Rae described the roller-coaster ride she had taken down the crushed shell road. After polishing off another glass of milk and part of a sack of cookies that he discovered in the cupboard, Brian loped up the stairs to his room and changed into jeans. Then he headed out back to the driveway to jack up the Ford and substitute the spare for the badly shredded rear tire.

Rae wanted to sob every time she caught sight of her broken headlight and the rest of the damage to her nice little car. But at least by the time Brian put the wrenches away, it was in running order again. Together they rode into town. He tagged along while she did the grocery shopping, all the while adding items to the basket that she wouldn't have bought herself.

"Keep it up with the munchies and there'll be nothing but exercise equipment under the Christmas tree for you this year," she warned.

Both of them worked off plenty of calories in the water later that afternoon. One of the best features of living where they did was the golden crescent of sand curving lazily up to their back garden. This private little beach was flanked on either side by leafy inlets, where twisted mangroves rooted almost at the water's edge. The entire stretch of coast alternated between these dark, inconspicuous coves, snaking sinuously inland toward the swamp country, and sunlit patches of beach, which snuggled between them like free-form chips of a mosaic.

Rae swam vigorously for almost half an hour, then flipped over onto her back to float leisurely in the foaming surf. Every weekend sailor in the county seemed to be out on the Gulf today, taking advantage of the light scudding breeze and cloudless sky. She wondered how in the world Simon Kirk had expected them to notice a strange craft in the midst of a crowd like that. For that matter, the boat he was looking for didn't have to be out on the Gulf at all. Any number of vessels could be concealed in the inlets lying to either side of the Travis property—or that of every other home owner up and down the coast for a hundred miles in each direction, as far as that went. A boat could slip out at night and back before dawn, unnoticed as a firefly in the daylight.

The notion caused Rae a vague uneasiness that she couldn't quite dismiss. She waded back to shore, Brian following, and dropped down on one of the oversized towels they'd spread across the sand. Pensively she reached for the tube of sun block to renew the protection on her fair skin. Now that she'd started thinking about it, it was impossible to close her eyes to the matted, junglelike vegetation only a shell's throw away.

Rae knew that the work of the cutters such as the one her brother served aboard most often consisted of rescue work. They were usually the first ones on the spot when a vessel or plane went down at sea. The Coast Guard also enforced maritime law, established safety standards for ships and small boats alike, gathered weather information, and backed up the Navy on joint operations. She had a hunch that Brian's branch of the service would be a natural when it came to the war against smuggling too.

"Do you run into many illegal aliens trying to slip into the country without authority?" she asked.

"Out on patrol, you mean? Within our own waters we'd most likely take them aboard and turn them over to Immigration," Brian said. "Farther out, we persuade them to head back to wherever they came from. There are always refugees of some war-torn country or other trying to make it to safety here in the States. Poor guys; you can't blame them for wanting a decent life. But there's always the chance that they're carrying diseases—not to mention other unsavory items we'd just as soon keep out."

He borrowed her tube of sun block and slathered a glop of it on his nose. A glance at the frothing waves prompted a question of his own. "Why? Spot someone out there you think ought to be corraled?"

"Of course not. But a border patrolman was out this way yesterday. He was asking Dad and me questions about unfamiliar boats. He's the one who brought up the illegals."

"Can't say I'm surprised. With the Enclave out there—"

Rae perked up her ears. Farther down in the Caribbean, the island known since the third voyage of Columbus as Alta Monte had recently acquired a new designation. Alta Monte's dictator, Felipe Muñoz, had thrown open the rugged, barren land to the brotherhood of worldwide terrorists, guaranteeing them sanctuary there no matter how barbaric their deeds elsewhere. Bombings, assassinations, insurrection—none of that mattered to Muñoz so long as they paid, and paid well.

The media had coined the term "Enclave" to refer to this stronghold of terrorism located not too many hundred miles south of America's shores. In the past few months ordinary travelers had been denied access to the small nation. Its university was closed, and island residents were prevented from leaving. From Dr. Hamilton's concerned comments on the subject, Rae knew he feared that members of Alta Monte's scientific community might have been coerced into working with the terrorists.

As if there weren't enough violence in the world already! Rae repressed a shudder. Her own work and that of her colleagues at the Avionics Lab was specifically aimed at safeguarding aircraft from explosive devices that might be placed aboard. That was what Project G.A.T.E. was all about. The acronym stood for Guardian Against Terrorist Encroachment.

She wasn't allowed to talk about the developments there, though, not even to her own brother. "Do you think that in addition to being used as a refuge, some of those cutthroats might be using the Enclave as a jumping-off spot?" she asked. "Leaving there to come . . . anywhere?"

Brian shrugged. "Your guess is as good as mine, Sis."

But from the studious way he avoided her eyes, Rae didn't think so.

Dan Travis had a pleasant surprise awaiting him when he returned home just before six. Not only was Brian there to greet him, but Rae had thick steaks barbecuing on the grill.

He accepted a frosty julep and settled himself at the picnic table within scenting distance of the barbecue. "Now this is what I call a welcome!" he exclaimed.

"Have a good day, Dad?" Rae added a skillet of mushrooms to sauté over the smoldering embers while Brian brought out plates, napkins, and silverware.

"Good and hot and good and busy." His grumble didn't sound unhappy. "If this weather continues, we're liable to get rich. Never saw so many darn-fool fishermen out in all my life."

"No sign of that strange boat Simon Kirk mentioned?"

"Honey, the Gulf was so full of strange boats that half of Cuba could have landed and nobody would have been the wiser," he declared wearily. "He'll have to do his own sorting out."

That was precisely the trouble, Rae thought. How could anyone hope to identify one suspicious craft from among the hundreds of innocent boats thronging the Gulf? Simon Kirk had set himself an impossible task—unless he had more concrete information than he was revealing.

Serves him right for being so secretive, she decided perversely. They had offered to help. Inspector Kirk would have only himself to blame if he never laid eyes on that phantom barge, or whatever it was he was after!

The air-conditioning was showing signs of pulling a brownout, due to the constant demands on the utility company's resources during the heat wave. Finally the Travis family had shut theirs down entirely.

"I don't know about you, but I'm about to suffocate." Brian tossed aside the copy of *Sports Illus-*

trated he'd been using as a fan. "Want to take another swim or go for a walk?"

"After this afternoon I'm still half waterlogged. I wouldn't mind a stroll, though, in case there's any chance at all of catching a breath of air." Rae stood up, using a tissue to dab at her damp forehead. "How can Dad sleep in this weather? I peeked in at him a while ago, and he was droning away like a motorboat in a high sea!"

It was only ten o'clock, but fishermen started their day early, and so did the people who provided them with supplies. Dan Travis was anticipating another busy day come tomorrow. He took few holidays this time of year. The hurricane season to come might last weeks or months. During that chancy period business was slack. The bulk of his living was earned while the weather was good and the fish were biting.

Rae sprayed herself liberally with mosquito repellent, then hunted out a pair of snakeproof boots. She was not unduly afraid of the reptile and insect life native to the low coastlands, but she believed in taking sensible precautions while walking outside in the evenings.

So did Brian, who wore Levi's and thick boots and a cool white cotton T-shirt. "Better bring the flashlight," she reminded him.

"Why? Expecting old Davy Crockett-dile to come nibbling at your ankles?" he teased.

The ancient, slow-moving gator had been almost a childhood pet. Whenever the opportunity arose, they had slipped away to visit the marshy pool where he drowsed. They'd thought it hilarious to name him after a famous frontiersman. Davy had devoured many a peanut butter sandwich in those days. Prudently neither Rae nor Brian had ever mentioned this scaly friend to their parents.

"I haven't seen Davy in years." Rae giggled. "I wonder if he's still in that old pool, or whether the moss has finally grown over him."

Brian threw out a challenge. "Let's find out."

"It's a long way," she demurred. "Besides, we never went there at night."

"I can find it. You're not afraid, are you?"

"Who, me? Afraid of old Davy Crockett-dile? Don't be silly!"

She couldn't back down in the face of her brother's dare, but tramping along the swampy, overgrown trail, Rae had to admit that the prospect of visiting the gator pool was considerably less alluring than it would have been fifteen years earlier. The sultry night air throbbed with bird cries, high-pitched and eerie. Small animals scampered into the undergrowth at their approach, and once a snake slithered across the path almost beneath their feet.

The house was about half a mile behind them when Brian suddenly switched off his flashlight.

"Did you hear something?" he whispered.

"Lots of things," Rae said. "I may move North in the morning!"

"Shhh, quiet. I didn't mean just birds or animals." Softfooted as a Seminole, he padded ahead.

Rae caught at his arm. "Brian, I'm not taking another step until you tell me what—"

"Listen!"

A staccato "dah-dah-dit" ricocheted through her ears. Brian hunched down; instinctively Rae dropped to one knee.

"What is that?"

"Morse code." Brian's whisper was so low she barely caught the words. "Somebody's operating a radio transmitter."

"Here? That's crazy! Why—"

"Stay put. Don't budge. I'm going to edge up a little closer and see if I can find out what's going on."

Before Rae could answer, he was gone. Too stunned to rebel, she watched the white blur of his T-shirt merge with the shrubbery. The transmitter chattered in snatches. Whenever the pulsating whine ceased, the silence seemed extra loud, as if even the wildlife had paused to listen for the next burst of signals.

That white shirt of her brother's made a perfect target, Rae thought nervously. She had no idea who the radio operator was or what his purpose in choosing such an isolated spot could be. However, the very fact that he was sending his message from the middle of a swamp long after dark was more than enough to brand him a suspicious character.

Even as she formed the thought, the chattering abruptly broke off. A sharp report whiplashed through the trees.

Brian streaked back down the path, making no attempt to soften his thudding footsteps.

"Run!" he ordered, grabbing her hand. "They're shooting at us!"

Rae didn't wait to be coaxed. She had been eager to leave the swamp since the moment they'd arrived. Now that bullets were added to the normal hazards, she wasted no time on questions. With Brian close behind her, she bolted down the tangled path.

A second bullet twanged overhead. It thudded dully into a tree a few feet over their heads. The person behind the rifle was starting to zero in. Fortunately the trail zigzagged, and the dense vegetation soon provided an adequate shield. Nevertheless Rae didn't even begin to slow down until they were in sight of the house.

"I've never been so frightened in all my life!" she panted when they were safely inside with the door bolted. "Why was he shooting at us?"

"He wanted privacy—or rather, *they* did. I caught a glimpse of two shadows. They spotted me too." Brian looked down disgustedly and picked a thorny leaf off his shirt. "If I'd had the sense to wear something less conspicuous, I might have gotten close enough to learn what they were up to."

"You couldn't understand the message?"

Brian had mastered Morse code back in Scouts and taken a refresher course in boot camp. "Sure," he said now and started for the phone. "What's the name of that border patrolman who was around yesterday asking questions?"

"Kirk. Simon Kirk." Quickly Rae located the notepad on which she had jotted his telephone number. She had been thinking of insurance forms when requesting it the previous day. Now it seemed he was needed in an official capacity.

As soon as the other man came on the line, Brian identified himself and touched on the high spots of the amazing encounter. His terse mention of the radio transmitter was enough to make Simon Kirk cut him off in midsentence.

"Hold it. That's enough over the phone," he interrupted. "The house where I'm staying is on the water too. I'll bring a motorboat up to your patch of beach as quick as I can. Meet me there."

Brian hung up and hurried upstairs to swap the offending T-shirt for something dark. He hustled down again four minutes later to find Rae pulling on an old denim jacket.

"Where do you think you're going?" he protested, as if he didn't know the answer to that one. "It's dangerous out there!"

"Ha! You dragged me off to meet an alligator without any qualms about danger, didn't you? Just try leaving me out of this!"

"Listen, Rae, that guy wasn't shooting skeet. He might still be skulking around, trying to find us."

"He'll be sorry if he does. I loaded Dad's shotgun." Rae handed the weapon to him and thrust a box of shells into her pocket. "Don't waste time arguing—come on! The sooner we get back there, the better our chances of catching that sniper."

"Okay, okay." Brian retrieved the flashlight and motioned his sister back while he played the beam around the garden. Nothing stirred, but from the water came the distant sound of a boat.

"Let's go."

They loped across the sand and waited at the low-tide mark until Simon Kirk had beached the motor-boat. Seconds later the three of them were on a first-name basis—more for speed and efficiency, the rueful thought hit Rae, than for friendship's sake.

"The message first. What did it say?" Simon demanded.

Brian fished a slip of paper out of his pocket. "A lot of gibberish. Here, I wrote down as much as I heard. It's in English—if that's what you could call it: 'Starlight. Winding road. Tennyson's gray. Straw figures.' The radio operator broke off there, and either he or his buddy started shooting. What crazy kind of code is that?"

"The toughest kind." Simon had the boat scooting back into the water the instant they climbed aboard. "Think you can find this place again?"

Brian nodded. "One of these little inlets chops right across the trail we took. The guys with the radio were on the opposite bank from us, which is probably the only reason I'm not walking around with a slug in my ribs right now."

Simon hugged the coastline, detouring twice around sandbars while Brian peered at each tiny channel swirling darkly inland. Rae sat motionless in the rear of the boat, marveling at their intentness.

Simon must have had dozens of questions he wanted to ask, yet so far not an unnecessary word had been exchanged.

We certainly stumbled onto something, Rae thought, watching what little moonlight there was spark highlights in Simon's dark hair. Tonight there was no gold eagle insignia to attract attention, no badge. But a holstered revolver hung from the belt around his waist. She noticed the flap was unbuckled. The lethal weapon could be drawn in a hurry, if necessary.

"Try here. This is about the right distance." The branch of the stream to which Brian pointed was all but invisible against the black curtain of trees. Only the eddying ripples where it emptied into the Gulf betrayed its presence.

Simon cut the throttle, dropping the motor throb to its lowest pitch. "Keep a lookout for roots and stumps," he ordered, half turning to let Rae know the instructions were for her. "Wouldn't be much fun to have to wade home from here."

No, and it wouldn't be a jolly experience if the men with the high-powered rifle were camped around the next bend waiting for them, either. Rae kept the notion to herself and scanned the inky surface of the water, alert for obstacles that might rip a hole in their boat. She hadn't forgotten that coming along had been her own decision. She was torn between hoping they'd be able to intercept their quarry, radio and all, and praying that they were long gone.

They had been chugging upstream for no more

than three or four minutes when Brian gave a satisfied exclamation. He pointed to a small clearing on the right.

"Hit it first try," he said softly, pleased with his navigating. He turned his head to peer at the opposite bank. "See the trail over there? I must have come within a half-dozen yards of the water when they spotted me."

To Rae's infinite relief there was no sign of anyone here now. Expertly Simon edged the boat up to the bank and looped the painter around the root of a mangrove. When it was securely tied, the three of them scrambled ashore.

At first the clearing appeared to be just another chunk of wilderness, devoid of any human trace. Almost at once, however, the flashlights the men carried picked out a square indentation where some heavy article had crushed the spongy earth. Trampled bootprints around the inch-deep depression testified to the fact that someone—two someones—had walked here recently.

Simon seemed to be measuring the sunken area with his eye, as if such a move would in time help him identify the weighty item causing it. Brian looked for cartridge casings, but there were none to be found.

It was Rae, hanging back, letting them take the lead, who made the discovery. A stray beam from one of the flashlights flickered across an object near the water's edge. Her eye caught the glimmer of glass.

Bending over, she scooped it up for a closer examination.

"Take a look." She handed the delicate-looking bulb to Simon. "This hasn't been here long enough to gather dust, let alone moss."

Simon's glance warmed with congratulation as he cupped the find carefully in his palm. "Good work," he said. "This confirms Brian's talk about a radio message and reinforces my hunch about what it was sent with. Looks like a tube from one of those big, old-fashioned shortwave sets."

"I know the sort you mean. Uncle Charley had one on his boat, remember, Bri?"

"Still does, far as I know. So do a whole lot of other people. They're bulky but reliable and have a heck of a range."

"And one of the few drawbacks to that sort of set was that the tubes blew every so often. You needed spares, especially if you had a special message and wanted to be absolutely sure it got through," Simon finished in a thoughtful tone.

With two of them having handled the small object, there was little hope of finding helpful fingerprints on the surface. Nevertheless Rae noticed that Simon tucked it away securely before continuing the search.

A careful combing of the area turned up no more pointers to whoever it was that had been operating the radio. Finally they gave up and climbed back into the boat. At Brian's suggestion they headed for the Travis house to talk things out over a cup of coffee.

Rae could think of at least a dozen questions she

wanted to ask, but she held her tongue, remembering Simon's tendency to keep his own counsel. She considered it a hopeful sign that he'd at least agreed to sit down and talk things over with them. That was only fair, in her opinion. Had it not been for Brian and herself, he never would have known about that radio or the weird message being beamed out over it.

Against a background of perking coffee, they settled themselves around the kitchen table. Simon looked tired, as though long hours on the job were beginning to catch up with him, but he gave a half grin at the sight of their intent faces.

"You two look as if you're about to burst. I admit I'm curious about a number of things myself. What ever possessed you to go hiking in a swamp at this time of night?"

"Believe it or not, we were looking for an alligator. Davy Crockett-dile, to be exact." Rae gave a sheepish smile of her own as she went on to explain. It faded as she added, "We were prepared against snakebite—but we never expected to be shot at."

"Who *were* those guys?" Brian asked pointedly.

"Don't you think I'd like to know?" Simon took the steaming mug Rae handed him and kept his eyes on her brother. "What's your guess about this whole affair?"

Brian had been expecting answers, not more questions. He echoed the discussion they'd had that afternoon. "We think it has something to do with illegal entries." He glowered across the table. "Your turn."

Simon's tone was solemn as he said, "I think it has something to do with illegal exits."

"Exits!" Rae felt swamped with confusion. "What would that have to do with the Border Pa—"

"We're only part of it. You might say the FBI included us in."

Stretching his long legs out under the table, Simon seemed to be considering where to begin and how much he could tell.

"In the past few months several unsettling incidents have taken place at different airfields along the Eastern seaboard," he said at last. "In a couple of cases it was actual aircraft that were placed at risk. Runway lights were tampered with at LaGuardia, and at a field near Washington, D.C., the control tower was sabotaged. Word was," he added in a quiet tone, "that a group of VIP's from Israel were due in that day. The plane in question landed safely, thanks to quick thinking on the part of a local cop, but the results could have been disastrous."

"You're talking about terrorists, aren't you?" Rae's face looked stiff with apprehension. "Groups of fanatics who believe in bombings rather than speeches to make their point. Were they caught? Was anything proven?"

"Yes, no, and no again," Simon answered her questions concisely. "There's very little doubt in anyone's mind that one group of radicals or another were responsible for each of these episodes. The Bureau's been keeping tabs on several suspected haunts of these people, and they've run across an interesting pattern. Time and again persons thought to be involved in this sort of attempted mayhem were observed heading south, often within minutes of planting the explosives, or whatever."

"South?" Brian's voice was one big question mark. "Can you be a little more specific than that?"

Simon gave a cynical laugh. "Do I have to be? All right; I'll lay it on the line. By a variety of routes and means of transportation, they're heading right down here to the lower Gulf Coast of Florida. Also," he added, finishing off his coffee with a gulp, "strong shortwave radio signals have been picked up twice in the past. They've been pinpointed as having come from somewhere in this area."

Danger to the Avionics Lab was uppermost in Rae's mind, but so far there seemed to be no threat posed to the installation simply because known terrorists routinely headed in this direction. Yet even the possibility of such conscienceless people lurking nearby was enough to send cold fingers of fear creeping across the back of her neck.

"Those signals," she said and found it amazing that her voice didn't seem to shake at all, "were they intended to reach a foreign ship?"

Simon shook his head. "No, the FBI has a theory that someone along this coast is running a ferry service. As you mentioned yourself, something the size of one of the cruise liners would draw instant comment. But a cabin cruiser would be the perfect solution. Since there are so many of them around, nobody's inclined to pay them any attention. Yet a forty- or fifty-footer has the range and power to take them exactly where they want to go."

"What about that weird code?" Brian asked. "All that stuff about 'Tennyson's gray' and the 'winding road'?"

"Whoever set up this operation is really clever." Despite the compliment there wasn't a trace of admiration in Simon's voice. "Especially with the use of computers, today's cryptographers have very little trouble deciphering a letter- or number-substitution code. But by using certain key phrases which simply mean something else, they've so far managed to slip their messages through without the gist of it being interpreted. 'Starlight,' for example, could refer to a date, a time, a latitude and longitude, or a specific person. Maybe any of those things, depending on its position within the message."

It was spooky. Rae hated the feeling that people with no respect for life or liberty continued to keep the upper hand over those who were struggling so hard to preserve those precious things. A sudden thought occurred to her.

"Simon, you said the signal had been pinpointed as having come from this part of Florida's coastline. Was—was it possible to tell from the direction of the transmission where the message was meant to be received?"

"I'd be surprised if you hadn't already figured that out for yourself." Simon's level gaze acknowledged the quick intelligence of the young woman seated across the table from him. "Just in case you haven't, though, there's an island a few hundred miles south of here named—"

"Alta Monte." Rae's voice came out in a groan. "The Enclave!"

Chapter Four

In spite of the late night they'd had the evening before and the fact that very little sleep was logged even when they finally turned in, both Rae and Brian were up shortly after their dad left for the bait-and-tackle shop next morning.

"Are you thinking what I'm thinking?" Rae was almost scared to look at the headlines of the fat Sunday paper Brian had just brought in from the front step.

"Probably," Brian admitted, worry crowding the usual merry sparkle out of those green eyes that both he and Rae had inherited from their mother. "All night long I kept wondering which of our airports might have been damaged or if a bomb had exploded on another jumbo jet."

Equally apprehensive thoughts had kept her tossing and turning for hours, Rae said. "According to Simon, those radio messages tie in to escape plans by terrorists who've been up to the worst sort of dirty work. The way he talked about a 'ferry service,' I figured that Morse-code message we interrupted last night with our search for Davy Crockett-dile was bound to be a tip-off to the Enclave to expect one of their people back as soon as they could cover the distance."

Setting aside the funnies and want ads and the rest of the bulky weekend newspaper, they spread the front section across the kitchen table. Though the front page had its usual quota of strife and scandal to report, nothing appeared, either there or in the pages that followed, to so much as hint at attempted sabotage of the sort they'd been expecting to see.

Did that mean someone had failed in his mission? From all that Rae had heard of the various terrorist organizations, blunders were not taken lightly. Orders were meant to be followed through, do or die.

She pushed down a shudder and opened the box of doughnuts Brian had insisted on adding to the shopping cart the previous day. It was ridiculous, she thought, to be letting this situation get to her. Whoever had sent that message from the nearby swamp must have been at least as shaken up as she and Brian at the unexpected encounter. Armed or not, they would surely never dare attempt to return. As for the message itself—

Well, it could have meant anything, she told herself. Anything! But at least it hadn't seemed to refer to another air-related disaster.

To keep her mind off such gloomy matters, she eventually left Brian dozing in the hammock slung across their screened veranda and drove on down to the wharf to keep her dad company in his shop. It was another spectacular day, slightly cooler than the last couple had been, but still plenty warm enough to prompt everyone who could to get out on the water where the fresh sea breeze provided some welcome natural ventilation.

"Is that the *Coral Belle* I see out there?" Rae stood on tiptoe, shading her eyes for a better look at the powerful cruiser anchored half a mile out. "I thought Jeff told me Friday that he had charters for the whole weekend."

Mr. Travis chortled. "He's got a party with him, all right. Came in first thing this morning for a bucket of bait with a Mr. and Mrs. Petrie with him, all set to go trolling for tarpon. An hour later he's back, putting in at the dock long enough to set Mr. Petrie ashore. Turns out the poor fellow gets seasick on any body of water bigger than a swimming pool. The missus, though, is still out there, getting her money's worth."

Rae rolled her eyes. Jeff must have been fit to be tied. Without a doubt, the next time she saw him she'd have to listen to another tale of woe about the inept amateurs who chartered his boat. Still, at the rates he charged for a day's hire, she couldn't really see what he had to squawk about. Although if Mr. Petrie had been *really* seasick—

She did her best not to laugh. Jeff was a good friend, and if he was a trifle intolerant of fishermen who weren't in his league, he at least didn't vent his spleen within their hearing. And more than once, she reminded herself, he'd listened patiently to her complaints about Alyssa Fairfax's high-handed attitude. It balanced out.

But having a friend such as Jeff wasn't at all the same as the sort of deep, adoring relationship her brother and Dana Webb enjoyed. Rae had this fact brought home to her for the umpteenth time when seeing the engaged couple together that evening. They planned to be married soon after the first of the year; in the meantime every minute Brian and Dana could snatch to be together was valued to its fullest. Both of them were younger than she by several years. What was the matter with her that she hadn't found that someone special of her own yet?

Generally Rae was a happy, well-adjusted person who felt quite content with the fulfilling life she led. She also made a habit of being honest with herself. It was Simon Kirk who had started her thinking along the lines of couples and wondering how she and he would match—as if she didn't already know! There was no future for them at all. Heavens, the first time he'd seen her, he'd come straight out with a warning about being too busy to pursue a social life.

Besides, she thought with a pang, he wasn't here to stay. But she most definitely was. Her home was here, and her job. Vitally important work. Project G.A.T.E. had a long way to go. She intended to stay and see it through.

During the next day and a half Rae did her best to put all thoughts of the attractive Simon Kirk out of her mind. There had been no need for him to swear Brian and herself to secrecy, she thought, slightly miffed that he'd apparently found it necessary to do so. They were both highly conscious of national security. Did he think that people with the kind of responsible jobs such as they held down were about to go blabbing all over town about a radio operator who played hide-and-seek in swamps and took potshots at innocent hikers?

Just before noon on Tuesday, Rae left Avionics to take her scratched and dented Ford in for repairs. She arrived promptly for her twelve-fifteen appointment. Even so, she found the mechanic not quite ready to devote his attention to the bodywork her car would need. He was still adjusting the trunk latch on a green sedan.

Rae couldn't help smiling in relief at the sight of the flawless paint job that had been given the car she'd rammed into the previous Friday.

"Did a good job, didn't he?" Coming up behind her, Simon showed that he was also gratified at the efficient and speedy repairs that had been made to his vehicle.

"He sure did," Rae agreed. "I'm hoping he can fix mine up just as nicely. I still have three more payments to make on it. Have you seen those bumper stickers on dilapidated autos: 'Don't laugh—it's paid for'? I'm afraid I couldn't even make that claim."

"It's gonna be fine, Miz Travis. Don't you worry your head on that score." Overhearing her woebegone statement, the mechanic hastened to set her mind at ease. "You might as well take the loaner this fellow's been driving. Bring it back in Thursday around five. By then I'll have your own car ready for you, good as new."

Simon handed her the keys to the tan Plymouth out front, then laid a hand on her arm to prevent her from leaving immediately. "It's lunchtime," he said. "If you haven't eaten yet, would you like to grab a bite with me?"

Rae wanted to; yes. But she had a feeling it wouldn't be a good idea. "Sure you can spare the time?"

With an expression every bit as grave as her own, Simon gazed back at her. "Yeah," he answered after a minute. "Provided we keep it down to hamburgers and fries. Which are you holding against me—the fact that I told you the first time we met that I didn't get much time off, or my asking you and your brother to keep what happened the other night to yourselves?"

She could feel the hot color rising, staining her chin and cheekbones and probably disappearing under her bangs. "Both," she snapped. "In my opinion, the request was as unnecessary as the statement. I don't talk out of turn, especially about confidential matters. And I didn't ask you to squander any of your precious hours on me."

"This one's being squandered right now while we stand here arguing," he pointed out reasonably. "Come on; there's a fast-food place across the street. If you're still mad by the time we're through eating, you can squirt the ketchup at me."

Rae pictured him with a vivid red stain smeared

across that tanned brow or dribbling off his rugged chin. That proved to be a mistake. She found herself focusing much too intently on those particular features, then taking in the others that made up his face. His eyes were a deep, velvety brown, framed with the kind of lashes most women would resent as being longer and thicker than their own. Even though it had a tendency to poke itself into other people's business, his nose was straight and thin. His mouth—oh, that was nice.

She looked away. "All right. But we'll have to hurry."

Once seated at the square yellow table with their plates in front of them and refreshing glasses of iced tea already half gone, each made an effort to put the other at ease. Rae told him how much fun she'd had going to school in Miami, which was where he hailed from. Simon said what a neat place Shell Bay seemed to be.

"Your dad was telling me before—ah, before you arrived home the other day—that you work for that big lab with the ten-foot fence around it," he remarked when he had tucked away half the hot, oniony, pickle-laden sandwich. "What do you do there?"

Rae masked a smile at his attempt at tact. What had he started to say? she wondered. "Before you came barreling into the driveway"? "Before your smashing entry"? Something of that sort, without a doubt.

"If people who work at the lab could talk about

what they do," she said sweetly, "there wouldn't be any *need* for a ten-foot fence around the place."

"Touché!" Simon grinned. "You're my kind of woman, Rae. You give as good as you get. And I'm sorry if I insulted you by reminding you to keep your mouth shut about what happened the other night. I should have known such a request wouldn't be necessary." He dragged a French fry through the ketchup, then looked up again before raising it to his mouth. "I'm not sorry about the other, though—about telling you that I didn't get much time off. Or rather, all I'm sorry about on that score was not phrasing it more tactfully. What I guess I was trying to say was that I wished I were under less pressure at the moment because for the first time in a long time I'd found someone I wanted to spend hours with. Days. Weeks. Not just minutes."

He meant it, Rae thought. She'd bashed up his car and treated him with cool disdain, and he hadn't backed off. Instead, he'd been honest enough to open his heart to her.

"Simon. . . ."

"What are you thinking?"

Rae bit her lip. "That I like your name. That I like *you.* But it—it isn't going to work. There are too many things in the way."

"Like what?"

"Jobs. My job. Your job." She met his gaze and found herself being drawn in, right into his thoughts, to the sincere, solid person inside. "I'm involved in something important at work. It isn't the sort of thing that can be set aside halfway through. And you—"

"I'm only here for a little while." He saw the hopelessness of it and fought it. "How about Saturday? If I put in twelve-hour days between now and then, I can—"

"Oh, Simon, I'd love to. I would." Rae swallowed hard and looked down at her plate, at the food growing cold while she battled the feelings that threatened to take over her common sense. "But I can't." She looked up again, seeing doubt on his face, and hurt. "Oh, please—don't look like that. I meant it. I would love to see you again, but Saturday—it's my boss's birthday. He's turning fifty. That's an awful milestone to reach all by yourself, so I arranged with my friend Jeff to use his charter boat and take Dr. Hamilton out fishing."

"What a nice thing to do!" One of Simon's hands came across the table and captured hers. The hard, lean fingers meshed with her own. She could almost feel the strength of character there, the sort of person that Simon Kirk was, deep inside. "Your Dr. Hamilton isn't married? No family at all?"

Rae shook her head. "Not anymore. Something happened— Do you remember about three years ago the jumbo jet that exploded in the air halfway across the Atlantic? Mrs. Hamilton and their two boys were aboard. The whole family had been looking forward to a European vacation for years, and then something came up, some experiment that Professor Hamilton and his class had been working on at the university—

An extra few days was needed to finish it off. So rather than cancel all the reservations, he sent his family on ahead and promised to join them in London. Only—"

"Only, a group of fanatics decided to announce their displeasure with events in the Middle East." Simon saw tears blur Rae's beautiful green eyes, and a number of things clicked into place. The reason Cole Hamilton was no longer a university professor. The sort of things he and Rae and others were working on in that lab behind the ten-foot fence. And the way she made him feel.

She was right about one thing, he thought. The job she was doing was vital. But she wasn't right about the other, about it not working between them. Somehow, someway, he was going to make it work.

"Friday, then. We'll do something Friday, okay? Didn't I see a poster about a dance they're having somewhere that night?"

"Uh-huh." Rae was grateful for the change of subject. "It's a benefit thing. The volunteer fire department is raising money for some new equipment, and various community organizations are donating the auditorium and the band and supplying refreshments."

"Sounds perfect." The details meant less than nothing to Simon. What counted was that for the first time he and Rae would be meeting by arrangement, rather than by accident. "I'll come for you at seven."

"Seven," Rae repeated. It was a promise.

* * *

The following morning Dr. Hamilton wandered into Rae's office at coffee-break time with a folded newspaper under his arm. "Have you seen this?" he asked.

Rae scanned the discreetly worded paragraph on page five that he pointed to. The item was datelined Kingston, Jamaica, and credited to United Press International. From an unidentified source on the island of Alta Monte, according to UPI, word had filtered through that a prominent aeronautical engineer had mysteriously disappeared. Local authorities were investigating the whereabouts of Manuel Villanova, forty-one. Renowned for his work both at Alta Monte's Francis Xavier University, now closed for renovation, and for military contractors in various spots around the Caribbean, the scientist had been missing for several days. Villanova was believed to have been under a severe strain lately due to his mother's chronic illness.

She raised an eyebrow. "That's a nice tongue-in-cheek touch about the university on Alta Monte being closed for 'renovation.' Everyone in the Western Hemisphere knows that the terrorists shut it down when Felipe Muñoz gave them free rein on the island."

"I knew him, you know," Dr. Hamilton said unexpectedly. "Villanova. He was a very reliable researcher, and half a dozen innovative safety features installed on military jets belonging to Mexico and Venezuela were credited to him."

"Sounds like someone we could use here," Rae observed. "Is he the sort of person who would crack under the strain of coping with an illness in the family?"

A trifle absently her superior cocked his head to one side and gave it some thought. "I wouldn't have said so, although there was no denying that he was devoted to his mother. As a child Manuel came down with a severe case of rheumatic fever. Señora Villanova defied the doctors who predicted that her son was going to die and nursed him so conscientiously that he did recover in spite of the odds."

The virulent fever had left the youngster bald, Cole Hamilton added. "When I met him at a symposium in Buenos Aires five or six years ago, there wasn't a hair on his head. Poor fellow. I often wondered why he didn't get himself a toupee. Except for the baldness he would have been a good-looking man."

"Well, that shortcoming didn't seem to bother Telly Savalas or Yul Brynner." Rae read the article a second time. "Did you get the impression that the reporter who wrote this item was implying that Manuel Villanova had escaped from the Enclave? That all this talk about being under a strain was just a cover-up?"

"That's the way it sounded to me. Very likely the people in charge there on Alta Monte these days were pressuring him to do the sort of work that went against his grain." Dr. Hamilton shook his head and refolded the paper. "Poor guy. It might be possible for him to hide with sympathizers for a day or two. After that. . . ."

This pessimistic prediction was not borne out, however. A longer article on Villanova's disappearance appeared in Thursday's paper. The subject was definitely of interest to the employees of the Avionics Lab. Even Alyssa Fairfax commented on it when standing behind Rae in the line waiting to exit that evening.

On Friday the story exploded onto the front page. President Muñoz had posted a sizable reward, payable in Swiss francs, for the capture of Manuel Villanova.

"Dead or alive, presumably." Rae's tone was grim. She didn't like to think of the treatment in store for the missing scientist if and when he was recaptured.

"Dr. Rausch thinks there's a chance Villanova might have made it to safety," Dana said, taking the salad off her tray and sliding into the seat next to Rae's in the cafeteria. "That's likely to be just a case of wishful thinking, however. I suspect the boss would like to have the man's services right here in the lab and is crossing his fingers it all works out somehow."

"Well, if they haven't found him by now, maybe they aren't going to. They've had time enough to search under every rock and behind every stalk of sugarcane on that island by now." Knowing what a high-calorie lunch was on the agenda for Dr. Hamilton's party the next day, Rae was sticking to cottage cheese and peaches this afternoon. With a decided lack of enthusiasm she took another bite and looked over at her brother's fiancée. "There's no chance

Brian will be home this weekend. We got a quick phone call last night saying the cutter had been assigned to some search-and-rescue maneuvers."

"Could that be linked to this missing scientist, do you think?" Dana's expression turned thoughtful. "Kind of beating the waves just in case he did get away in a boat?"

"Who knows? The captain probably didn't tell Brian one way or another—and even if he had, he'd never have been indiscreet enough to repeat information like that over the phone."

This comment had the effect of turning Rae's thoughts to Simon Kirk, the man who had cautioned her to keep her lip buttoned on a certain matter and only days later apologized for having done so. He'd just been doing his duty, she knew. But it pleased her that he recognized that she really was a responsible person who could be trusted with a secret.

She hadn't said anything even to Dana about her date tonight. A hunch that she couldn't explain kept her from saying his name out loud. He wasn't going to be in the area very long, and she didn't want her friends getting the idea he was important to her and then feeling sorry for her later, after he'd left.

When the time came, she'd face that disappointment alone.

On the way home Rae picked up the cake she'd ordered from the bakery, stopped at the market for a half gallon of Rocky Road ice cream and enough frying-chicken pieces to satisfy several large appetites, and added a three-bean salad and a big plate of deviled eggs from the deli. The bakery provided yeasty rolls just out of the oven.

How horrified her grandmother would have been, Rae thought as she stowed away all the goodies when she arrived home. The tradition of Southern hospitality, which the first Rachel Travis had always maintained, declared that all foods should be lovingly prepared at home, from scratch, and served in the dining room to the accompaniment of the good dishes and cloth napkins. But that Rachel didn't have a job that kept her away from home nearly ten hours a day, in addition to a house to help keep up. Rae and her dad both pitched in to handle the domestic side of their lives, but neither of them had time to spend an entire afternoon preparing dinner.

She slid a couple of gourmet TV dinners into the oven, set the timer, and dashed upstairs to change out of the tailored outfit she'd been wearing all day. When the doorbell rang at five minutes to seven, she was clad in a lemon-yellow dress of lovely polished cotton. Looking and dressing like a Southern belle for the important man in one's life was a tradition that still hadn't gone out of style, thank goodness.

One look at Simon Kirk standing on the step, and Rae knew her instinct hadn't exaggerated.

He *was* the important man in her life.

On the way to the benefit dance their conversation had centered around such ordinary, unimportant topics that Rae guessed Simon was making an effort as great as her own to keep the pull that seemed to be drawing them together from getting out of hand. Any time a future event was accidentally mentioned—the Shell Fair up at Sanibel, which Rae looked forward to attending every March, or the Christmas boats parade, so popular up and down the coast during the holidays, or even the Labor Day picnic her father's lodge sponsored—Simon's expression grew still and tight, and he changed the subject in a hurry.

He knew he wasn't going to be around when any of those occasions arose, Rae thought with a flash of intuition. Simon didn't want to become any more deeply involved with her than he already was. He knew as well as she did that there wasn't any future for them.

When they arrived at the auditorium, they found that the lights had been turned down low and the decorating committee had done an excellent job of providing a romantic atmosphere. Rae was lost from the first slow ballad, when Simon put his arms around her to draw her close. She tried to fight it, in desperation even raising the subject of the radio tube she had found by the bank of the inlet six nights earlier. No luck, Simon said, in tracing the source of the tube's replacement so far. Obviously he had no desire to spend what little time they had together discussing the matter he'd been assigned to investigate.

The dance floor was crowded with dozens of couples. Even Jeff Carter was there, wrapped around a spectacular blonde who seemed fascinated by his every word. Rae closed her eyes, letting the lean strength of Simon's arms surround her. Her left hand brushed across the hard-bunched muscles of his shoulder as the music spun around them in slow circles. She wanted to shut out the sight of everyone and everything that might intrude on this bittersweet interlude.

It was something else that shattered the spell. At about ten o'clock the band members stood up to take a well-earned break. Rae had just started to suggest that they find a cozy table for two on the sidelines when a sharp beeping sound from Simon's jacket pocket made her jump and bite back the words.

His jaw tightened. In haste he fished out a small electronic pager and flicked his thumbnail across a button to silence the intrusive racket.

"I need to make a phone call." Clamping his hand around hers, Simon towed her along, apparently reluctant to be separated from her for the few moments remaining of their abbreviated evening.

Rae made no attempt to listen in on the terse dialogue between Simon and the party he dialed. The name he said first—Norm—indicated he was talking to his brother officer.

After a brief, low-voiced exchange, he hung up and swung back to face her. The look in his dark eyes was unmistakable. He was at least as disappointed as she was that their evening was being brought to a premature close.

"I'm sorry."

"Me too." She managed a smile and stiffened her

shoulders to make up for the fact that it wasn't a very convincing one. "You have to go, huh?"

"Yes, and right now too." Her question had the effect of starting him on his way toward the door.

He still hadn't let go of her hand. By tugging, Rae got his attention. "If it's that much of a hurry, you won't want to waste time taking me home."

Simon swung back to her, angry. She wasn't sure at what. "There's a good-sized boat creeping up the coast without any running lights showing. The chance that it's the one I've been looking for is a hundred-to-one shot, but—"

"But you can't take the risk of ignoring it. Go on, Simon. Duty calls. I know any number of people here tonight. This is my hometown, remember? I'll be just fine without you."

She whirled and stalked past him, but not before she'd seen the stricken look on his face. It should have stopped her, but it didn't. Regret didn't conquer anger until she'd gotten halfway across the room. By then it was too late. The doorway was empty when she looked back.

Chapter Five

The sun, a dazzling red-orange ball in the sky, hung low over the land to the east when Rae and her father chugged up to the public wharf early on Saturday. Dan Travis balanced the motorboat while his daughter climbed out, then he handed her the picnic basket. With that safely resting on the pilings, they next brought ashore the box containing the lavishly decorated cake.

"Hope Jeff hurries." Rae tilted down her sunglasses, gazing anxiously north in the direction of the marina where his cruiser was normally berthed. "I'd like to get all this stuff out of sight before Dr. Hamilton arrives."

Already the day gave signs of being another scorcher. Rae wore jeans and a sleeveless cotton top she'd purchased during a weekend jaunt to Walt Disney World up near Orlando a few months earlier. She'd put on the gaily patterned top to remind herself of that happy time and take her mind off what had happened the night before. She was determined not to spoil Dr. Hamilton's treat by giving in to the nagging ache in her heart.

Within a few minutes, the sleek bow of the *Coral Belle* slid gracefully up to the pier. Jeff Carter, a white skipper's cap tilted rakishly back atop his sun-bleached hair, lowered the anchor with a splash and nimbly hopped down to the weatherbeaten plankings.

"Hi." His sky-blue eyes narrowed in surprise as he caught sight of Rae standing on the pier alone. "Don't tell me I'm going to be lucky enough to have you all to myself today."

"Get that wolfish gleam out of your eye and help me stow these provisions out of sight before my boss shows up." Rae was an old hand at fending off Jeff's persistent advances. Sometimes she thought he persevered in the flirtation just to keep in practice, though heaven knew there were dozens of attractive women around who wouldn't have minded listening to his silver-tongued flattery.

Muscles rippling in his bronzed forearms, Jeff hoisted the box and basket aboard and carried them down to the galley. He had just emerged on deck again when a mini motor home pulled into the near end of the parking lot. Cole Hamilton climbed out of the cozy little rig whose refrigerator had never once given him vapor-lock problems. He strode down the pier toward the spot where Rae was waiting, looking vaguely astonished.

"Rae, when you said we were going fishing, I figured I was due for a ride in your family motorboat. I never expected you to hijack an ocean liner!"

The sleek, forty-six-foot cabin cruiser was an elegant sight, Rae admitted. Delighted with the way her birthday surprise had started out, she introduced the two men.

"Pleasure to meet you, sir." Jeff welcomed the older man aboard with such easy charm that there was no doubt at all how he managed to be so successful in the charter business. He might not care much for the majority of his passengers, but he knew how to show them a good time.

Jeff gave his guest the grand tour, pointing out the fighting chairs at the vessel's stern and the assortment of heavy tackle neatly stowed in the side compartments. "Rae tells me you enjoy fishing. Have you ever gone after the big ones?"

"Tarpon?" Dr. Hamilton gave a wistful grin. "Afraid not. I used to take my sons out on the lake years ago, where we pulled in a few trout, but that's the extent of my expertise."

"Well, we'll see if we can't help you hang one today." With an encouraging smile Jeff turned to manipulate the automatic anchor hoist, then got the *Coral Belle* underway.

Rae shot him a grateful smile. She had wanted this to be a very special day for one of her favorite colleagues, and Jeff was certainly doing his part to be cooperative. Revving up the powerful engine, he headed west until the Florida coastline was only a hazy blur on the horizon, then angled in a southerly direction, shifting the cruiser from spot to spot in search of a likely school of fish.

After several hours' trolling in various locations with no luck at all, Dr. Hamilton surprised everyone, himself included, by hooking a fast-moving streak that all but tore the rod from his hands. He tightened his grip, hanging on while Rae and Jeff both shouted encouragement, playing the fish with every bit of skill he could muster.

At the end of a hard-fought battle, the fish was finally hauled aboard. "Hey, doc, you got a beauty!" The oversized snook was held up for everyone's admiration while Jeff estimated its weight. "This baby ought to go nineteen, twenty pounds. Make a great trophy, huh?"

I couldn't have thought of a better birthday celebration with a year's advance notice, Rae exulted. Jeff, the weather—even the fish were cooperating!

It had been with crossed fingers that she'd brought her camera along. Now she captured several shots of Cole Hamilton proudly displaying his prize catch. Afterward, leaving the men on deck, she slipped down to the galley.

A few minutes later she maneuvered up the short, narrow flight of steps, carefully balancing a laden tray, and proceeded to spread the lavish picnic lunch out at the stern end of the cruiser. The cake she left below, unwilling to risk a trip up the gently heaving ladder with the beautifully frosted confection in her hands.

"Luncheon is served," Rae announced grandly, pointing to the feast anchoring the paper tablecloth against the breeze. "Unless you two would rather dine on Moby Dick over there."

Dr. Hamilton all but hugged the scaly creature he had decked. "You're suggesting we eat my glorious fish? Never!"

"Then you'd better come and get it!"

Both men tucked away gargantuan meals. The fresh sea air had left Rae with an enormous appetite too. Thankful that she had gone easy on the calories the day before, she found herself taking second helpings of everything.

After giving the main course time to settle, she headed below once again. Drawing Jeff aside while Dr. Hamilton leaned back in replete satisfaction, she asked him to bring the guest of honor down in about five minutes. "It will take me that long to light the candles."

The timing was perfect. Rae had just laid aside the last charred match when footsteps descended and the men joined her in the compact galley.

"Surprise!" she and Jeff shouted simultaneously. The two of them burst into a rousing rendition of "Happy Birthday to You."

Cole Hamilton's mouth fell open. Visibly moved by her thoughtfulness, it took him a moment to get his emotions under control. Glimpsing the suspicious sparkle of moisture in his eyes, Rae provided a diversion by suggesting he make a wish and blow the candles out before the frosting melted.

The sentimental moment was safely skirted. Dr. Hamilton took the knife Rae extended toward him, handle first, and ceremoniously cut the first slice. But he couldn't quite eliminate the hoarseness from his voice when he looked down at the symbol of his fiftieth birthday.

"A fish *and* a cake. It's too much!"

Fishing after this was an anticlimax. Grumbling that their off-key singing had probably scared away every fish for miles around, Jeff suggested that they venture ahead in search of "the big ones." Dr. Hamilton was happy to fall in with any plans the others cared to make. After noticing Jeff glance at his wristwatch, however, Rae found an opportunity for a discreet word with him.

"You've been awfully generous with your time already," she said, well aware of what the usual charge would have been for a day's rental of the cruiser. "I doubt that anything can top the pleasure we've already given him. Maybe we'd better head back in before we use up all your gasoline—and your patience too."

"Nope." Jeff shook his handsome head. "A deal's a deal, my sweet—a day's charter in exchange for a great lunch. Besides, I'm enjoying myself. Your friend is a nice guy. Let's see if we can't find him a tarpon and really give him a day to remember."

The *Coral Belle* cruised at high speed for half an hour or so, eating up the knots, then purred to a stop under Jeff's adroit handling of the controls.

"I can't promise anything, but Archie Fraser let slip the fact that he hit a fabulous school out here yesterday." Jeff's reference was to another charter captain whom Rae knew slightly. "Fish often stick around the same spot for several days, so we might be in luck. I'll break out the heavy tackle."

While Jeff attached strips of mullet to the barbed hooks, Rae and Dr. Hamilton positioned themselves in the big, swiveling fighting chairs at the boat's stern and attempted a few practice casts with the sturdier gear.

"Better cinch your safety belt," she warned Dr. Hamilton. "These fish have been known to weigh in at over two hundred pounds. A quick jerk and you might find yourself treading water."

He enthusiastically buckled up, and she followed suit. But Rae's own practice casts were halfhearted, to say the least. Her suggestion that they go back early had not been entirely altruistic. All morning long she had determinedly kept her attention focused on the here and now. With this lull, her thoughts persisted in reverting to the evening before and the hours she had spent with Simon.

Even now, many hours later and a hundred miles out in the Gulf, Rae wanted to bang her head against the *Coral Belle*'s railing for the lack of tact she'd shown. Sure, she'd been disappointed when the date she'd looked forward to all week had come to a screeching halt. But she'd known from the very beginning that with Simon duty came first. All she would have had to do was say, "Look—my neighbors, Ed and Mary Brannigan, are here. They never stay anywhere late because they have to get the babysitter home by eleven. I'll ride with them and see you . . . well, whenever."

She hadn't, though. She'd let him go with the impression that she could find some other man twice as appealing as he was who'd keep her there, dancing until the wee hours. It would be a long time before she forgot the look on Simon's face as she stalked past him. It was also likely to be a very long time before she saw him again—if ever.

At that point it would have taken something spectacular to yank Rae's attention away from the events of the evening before. Particularly today she had very little interest in fishing. She'd only buckled herself into the fighting chair to give good example to Dr. Hamilton, and the practice casts had been nothing more than a way of killing time until Jeff and her colleague decided they'd had enough of the open sea and decided to head for home. But suddenly the spectacular happened.

The seat belt saved her a swim, at least. Trolling her strip bait back and forth across the glassy surface of the water, Rae was suddenly catapulted forward as a violent tug yanked her shoulders half out of their sockets. The next instant a huge silvery fish exploded into the air.

"Tarpon!" Jeff shouted. "Give him room. Don't try to haul him in fast or you'll snap the line."

Mustering every ounce of strength in her slender arms and legs and back, Rae heaved the rod upright and reeled furiously before dipping the tip toward the fish again. Both Brian and her dad were expert fishermen. She had listened to enough of their exploits to know that these pumping maneuvers were the only way to boat a game fish as large as this one.

Again and again the tarpon spurted out of the water, then crashed shudderingly back beneath the waves. Rae gave line and fought to regain it. Each wind of the reel seemed like a major victory. Her left wrist began to swell from the effort of gripping the heavy rod. Every tendon in her shoulders felt as if it were on the verge of snapping. In the heat of battle Rae was almost oblivious to these discomforts.

She was going to boat that fish by herself or collapse in the attempt!

Dr. Hamilton had pulled his line out of the water the instant the bait was taken on hers to avoid the danger of tangling them together. He had leaped out of his own chair to hover excitedly near the rail, roaring encouragement while he hopped from one foot to the other. From the cockpit, where he was directing the cruiser, Jeff bellowed advice.

Suddenly the foam around the great silver tarpon boiled with renewed fury. Rae gasped in horror at the sight of two ugly black fins knifing toward her catch.

"Sharks!" Jeff turned the wheel, but he was helpless to avert the attack.

A moment later the line went slack. Wordlessly Rae handed the rod to Jeff and turned away from the sapphire waves with their frothings of foam.

"Tough break. That one would have gone for a record!"

"You darned near had him," Cole Hamilton chimed in sympathetically.

"At least I have two witnesses to help me brag about the one that got away." Rae managed a feeble smile. Tomorrow, she thought, she was going to ache in every joint. In fact, she already did. "Your luck is bound to be better than mine," she said. "Let's get away from this spot, and— Jeff, what's the matter?"

From his intent expression it was clear that something had made Jeff decidedly uneasy. "I don't like the way those sharks are acting," he growled. "Something has them licking their chops. Not the tarpon. Look at them turn up their noses at it. They're after juicier game."

The flesh of the huge game fish was considered much too tough and poorly flavored for humans to eat, but Rae had never heard of sharks turning up their ugly blunt noses at a meal of any kind. She shielded her eyes from the glare while Jeff loped across the deck and grabbed a pair of binoculars. Rae could feel the tension in his stance as he focused the lenses. Scanning the near horizon, she caught her breath as something, something that was not a fish, wavered into her line of vision.

Dr. Hamilton saw it at the same instant, but his eyesight wasn't keen enough to identify the low silhouette.

"I don't believe it!" Next to Rae, Jeff's incredulous words came out in a gasp. "Either that's a rowboat, or I've been out in the sun too long!"

Thrusting the binoculars into Rae's hand, he

sprang forward to activate the cruiser's controls. "There doesn't seem to be anyone in it, but I'm going to take a closer look, anyway."

Tension had increased to an almost unbearable state as the three people on the deck of the big boat strained to see what lay ahead in the water. In the past few minutes Rae had practically forgotten the disappointment of losing the tarpon. Like the men with her, she leaned forward intently. Hundreds of fathoms of blue water lay beneath their keel. The Florida coast had long since disappeared from sight, and it was a very long way to the nearest point of Mexican territory, the long, curving sweep of the Yucatán Peninsula. The closest island was Cuba. Below that less-than-cordial nation, to the south and west, lay hundreds of miles of open sea.

A rowboat! Clear out here?

Foam churned in the *Coral Belle*'s wake. The pulsating twin engines sent the cruiser scudding along at a rapid clip. From the port bow Rae glimpsed an ominous black fin before they outdistanced the shark.

"Jeff, you were right!" Rae exclaimed three minutes later. "It *is* a rowboat!"

Drawing far enough astern so that the wash from their vessel would not capsize the rowboat, Jeff jockeyed as near as he dared before cutting the motors.

Dr. Hamilton pointed to the motionless figure slumped across an oar. "Is— Do you think he's alive?"

"Miracles do happen, I suppose." Jeff snatched a pistol from a recess under the dash and with quick, efficient movements crammed shells into the cylinder. "We have to get rid of the competition before we can get near enough to find out, though. Stand clear."

Rae caught her breath, watching him take careful aim at the sharks milling avidly around the small boat that was dead in the water. The phrase as it crossed her thoughts had an ominous sound to it. She tugged Dr. Hamilton back, murmuring a warning about bullets possibly glancing off the hard surface of the water to ricochet back at the cruiser.

Jeff's first shot missed; the second provoked a whirlpool of tail-lashing fury. By the time he paused to reload, the marauding sharks had thrashed out of range. But they'd be back, the first instant they dared.

"Keep a lookout." He thrust the pistol into Rae's hand. "I'm going to find out whether that guy's still alive. Even if he isn't— Listen, if the sharks start edging back, fire into the air. The noise alone will probably scare them off."

Tossing a coil of rope into the dinghy, Jeff operated a pulley device to lower it over the side. Moments later he was dropping down, catlike, into the little boat. A dozen strokes of the paddle carried him across to the aimlessly drifting rowboat. The others watched, hoping against hope, as he bent over the prostrate form.

"He's still breathing!" came the welcome shout.

Rae exhaled in a whoosh, aware for the first time that she had been holding her breath. Her relief was shared by Dr. Hamilton, who swabbed his brow and sighed audibly.

Then began the painstaking process of transferring the inert man from rowboat to dinghy, from dinghy by rope up the side of the cruiser. There, four hands waited to haul him gently to safety. Jeff climbed the rope and fell onto the deck, panting from exhaustion.

"Heavier than he looked."

"Jeff, getting him aboard was an almost impossible feat of brawn and courage." Afraid that his strength might give out, Rae tried to persuade him to rest for a minute. Within seconds, though, he had struggled up to join the others as they crouched over the limp figure lying frighteningly still on the deck.

Rae's kind heart was touched by the man's appearance. A week's growth of beard stubbled his jawline. He wore an old straw hat, but raw patches of sunburn had nevertheless blistered his complexion. His shirt looked to have once been of good quality. Now the material was tattered and streaked with grime, as was the rest of his clothing.

She pressed a glass to his lips, dribbling a few drops of water down his throat while Dr. Hamilton felt for a pulse. The man's arms suddenly flailed, and his eyes fluttered open. A look of fear blanched his skin. He tried to rise, but the effort was too great.

"It's all right. You're safe now," Rae murmured reassuringly. How she wished Simon were here! Practical courses in Spanish were part of every border patrolman's training. He'd be able to talk to this poor soul, who probably didn't understand a word she was saying.

The man made no attempt to speak in any language at all. Instead, he continued to stare apprehensively at his rescuers, taking in Jeff Carter's vast, macho physique, Rae's anxious countenance. Dr. Hamilton's mild features seemed to spark a question in his mind; again and again his eyes drifted back to fasten on the scientist's face.

Suddenly the ensign flapping off the stern of the cruiser caught his attention. A sob of thanksgiving wracked his body as he gazed at the unfurled glory of the Stars and Stripes.

"Americans?" he asked in disbelieving wonder. "You are Americans?"

"Doggone right," Jeff affirmed. Rae's vigorous nod added reassurance.

"Then I have won! I am free!"

Despite their combined efforts to keep the half-delirious man from using up what remained of his slim store of strength, he insisted on struggling up to a sitting position and reaching forward to clasp their hands.

The battered straw hat slipped off his head. A head completely bald.

Dr. Hamilton's mouth fell open. "I don't believe it!" It was hard to tell whether shock or delight was uppermost in the stunned exclamation.

Rae could only stare and hope, remembering the conversation that had taken place in her office earlier that week.

It seemed that Jeff was the only one who had no idea of what the sudden consternation was all about. "You guys look like you've seen a ghost!"

"No," Rae said. "I think it's one of those miracles you were talking about a while ago."

"This is absolutely astounding," Cole Hamilton murmured in awe. "Millions of square miles of ocean, hundreds of boats keeping an eye out for him, and—"

"And *what?*" Jeff was beginning to sound rattled.

"And thanks to you, Jeff, we're the ones who managed it," Rae told him. "We've just found Manuel Villanova!"

Chapter Six

The rescued man seemed flabbergasted that they knew who he was. At first he shrank back in fear, keeping a wary eye on the other three, as though they might decide to return him to his rowboat and head him in the opposite direction. It took repeated assurances to convince him that was not their intention at all.

They did what they could to make him comfortable, all the while holding back their eager questions in view of his weakened condition. Rae dabbed soothing lotion on his sunburned face and ran down to the galley for a dish of the ice cream she and her two companions had been too full to eat earlier. This, she reasoned, would slide down his parched throat much more easily than more solid food.

Jeff, meanwhile, got the dinghy back aboard. By now the menacing shark pack had caught up with the cruiser, and the decision was made to simply abandon the rowboat that had been Manuel Villanova's stalwart transportation on his flight to freedom. Cole Hamilton stowed away the heavy tackle they'd been using to troll for tarpon. He waited until the *Coral Belle* was under way back to Shell Bay at top speed before lowering himself to a sitting position on the shaded portion of the deck next to where the refugee from the Enclave was resting.

"You look very familiar to me," Rae heard Villanova say as she brought over another cushion for Dr. Hamilton to sit on.

"It would not be surprising if you didn't remember me at all." Tactfully Dr. Hamilton mentioned that their only previous encounter had taken place several years before, at a symposium in Buenos Aires. "We both worked for universities, and our cultures were very different. But I like to think that we scientists inhabit a special kind of world where ideas are more important than national boundaries."

"I could not agree more. It is Hamilton, is it not? The professor who demonstrated how ailerons and elevator cables on an aircraft could be modified to assume glider functions in case of loss of power? My dear friend, your theory influenced my own research in many ways."

As she listened to the two men talking about the specialty that interested them above all else, Rae was impressed by Manuel Villanova's excellent grasp of English. Spanish, of course, was his native tongue, yet he managed the technical terms with no hesitation whatsoever. Scientists really did share a special world, she thought. She herself was well schooled in German, a language that scientists and technicians often found invaluable, and she had studied enough

French to be able to read the scholarly treatises in that language that sometimes crossed her desk. When attempting to speak French, however, she found it hard to get the accent right.

Jeff set the cruiser's automatic pilot. While the sleek vessel ate up the knots with an effortless roar of her powerful motors, he came back to join Rae at the starboard railing.

He still looked a trifle dazed at this latest turn of events. "So that's the missing VIP the newspapers have been posting bulletins about! At first I figured he must be some sort of nut. How many people go paddling around in the Gulf with only a compass and a dry water can?"

"There wasn't even an engine in that boat?" Rae looked back over her shoulder. "That must be some current, to help him maneuver this far north on muscle power alone!"

They had traveled more than halfway back to port before Manuel Villanova spoke of the motivation prompting his desperate escape.

"For years, as you must know, our island has been dominated by a tyrant, a harsh dictator who cares little for his people." Leaning back with his head cushioned on a pillow, he shuddered at the plight of his fellow citizens. "But Alta Monte was my mother's beloved homeland. Since she could not bring herself to leave, I, too, felt bound to stay on. She was a wonderful woman, my mother. There was nothing I would not have done for her."

Cold fingers touched Rae's heart. His usage of the past tense seemed ominous.

"Early this year the dictator went right over the edge and showed how unfit to govern he really is," the refugee continued. "Imagine the shock of citizens like me when without warning he threw Alta Monte open to the terrorist organizations of the world. What did the price he demanded matter to such as the PLO and the IRA? They think nothing of hijacking planes and armored cars and kidnapping millionaires for ransom. Because they needed a secure base in this hemisphere, they jumped at the offer Felipe Muñoz made them. Under their regime no one else was allowed to leave. My mother and I were trapped, along with thousands of our countrymen."

"And then they closed the university," Dr. Hamilton recalled.

"Of course. Undoubtedly they feared an uprising of the students. You know how hotheaded the young can be," Villanova said wryly. "Look at what happened in China recently. They knew that a similar rebellion on Alta Monte was sure to attract more adverse attention than even they were used to—and perhaps prompt the Organization of American States to impose sanctions against the island."

"But, my friend, what of your research?"

Manuel Villanova's eyes were stark with memories of what had been demanded of him. "I was ordered to find new ways to destroy aircraft, rather than work on ways to make them safer. I would have let them stand me up against a wall and open fire rather than help them in their goal, but . . . but there was my mother to consider. For some time now she has not been well. It is well known the devotion I bear for her, and so the first thing I was told, in dreadful detail, was what would happen to this beloved woman if I did not cooperate."

Rae wanted to weep for the man who had been faced with this fearsome dilemma. "Your mother. . . ."

"She died. Ten days ago." Villanova shook his head. "Or thereabouts; I have lost track of time. Drifting as I did, the hours and days all blurred together. But yes, my mother died. Before they learned of this, I took the first opportunity that came my way to attempt an escape. The boat had been my uncle's. It was old but seaworthy. I dared pack nothing for fear of being seen carrying it down to the shore. I stuffed a few items of food in my pockets, filled a garden can with drinking water, and started out with only an old compass as a guide. I still cannot believe I reached this point safely."

"What a story!" Jeff muttered, stunned at the daring of his new passenger. He put an arm around Rae's shoulders, turning her with him to look out to sea where their conversation would be swallowed up by the wind and the sound of the engines. "You don't think the Immigration authorities will turn the poor guy back, do you?"

"Not a chance." Rae remembered what Brian had said about refugees being handed over to Immigration when the Coast Guard picked them up in U.S.

waters. But this was a very special case. She had a hunch some intelligence agency would have plenty of questions for Manuel Villanova about the ruthless new inhabitants of the Enclave. But eventually, she had no doubt, he would be granted asylum.

"I'm sure they'll welcome him with open arms," she added. "From what Dr. Hamilton said the other day, he's a brilliant engineer. Boeing or Lockheed or—well, any number of aeronautical firms around the country would be delighted to offer him a position." *But not if Dr. Rausch got his request in first.* Rae kept this thought to herself, of course. Mentioning the sort of work that was done at the Avionics Lab or the type of scientific talent actively recruited for positions there was absolutely taboo. It didn't stop her from drawing her own conclusions, however. Particularly since Dana had come right out and said just a few days earlier that her boss would give a great deal to secure the services of a brilliant design engineer such as Manuel Villanova.

And what the director of the lab wanted, he usually got. The safety of the nation's aircraft was being given top priority in Washington these days.

Villanova's professional future would eventually be a matter for him and the powers-that-be to decide. Rae was concerned about his immediate future—what would happen when they brought him ashore. She felt sure some formalities would be necessary. After all, the man was a citizen of another country, and his impromptu arrival was being made without a passport in hand.

"Listen, Jeff, it would probably be a good idea to keep our entry as low-key as possible." She looked back over her shoulder at the two professors who were still talking shop. "That ghastly sea voyage was bound to have taken its toll on the poor guy; for sure he doesn't want to be facing a barrage of newspaper reporters before he has his strength back. Besides. . . ."

"Besides, the guy's an illegal alien." Jeff laid an even larger problem on the line. "Our first move had probably better be to call the police."

She shook her head decisively. "No, this really doesn't belong in their jurisdiction. It's Immigration who'll need to deal with Señor Villanova." It occurred to her suddenly that the Border Patrol was one of the main enforcement agencies within the Immigration and Naturalization Service of the Department of Justice. This was something she wouldn't have known if she hadn't been interested enough in Simon Kirk to study up on the agency he served with. Now she was mighty glad she had taken the trouble.

Whether Simon Kirk wanted anything more to do with her or not, she knew for a positive fact that he wouldn't turn his back on anything he considered his duty. And this was definitely right up his alley.

"I know someone who works for one of their branches. He's local." Temporarily local, Rae added to herself with a pang. "I'll run to Dad's shop and give him a call the instant we reach the wharf. Till we hear what he has to say, it probably wouldn't be a good idea for anyone else to go ashore."

"Whatever you think best." When it came to his boat or anything to do with sport fishing and the charter business, Jeff liked to be totally in charge. His attitude made it clear that this problem they were discussing now was one he didn't want to have to deal with.

It was very late afternoon by the time the *Coral Belle* eased up to the pier. Jeff threw a painter out and tied up at one of the pilings. Then he walked back across the deck to keep the other two men company while Rae hopped up onto the worn plankings and streaked toward Dan Travis's bait-and-tackle shop. She had reason to be grateful for the long hours her dad worked summer and winter; the shop was still open despite the fact that he'd started before six.

He was busy with a customer when she hurried inside. Rae gave a quick wave, announced she wanted to use the phone, and marched back to the cluttered little office in the rear of the shop. Moments later the man who had occupied the forefront of her thoughts for much of the afternoon came on the line.

"Simon, it's Rae. We just returned from that fishing trip I told you about."

"I see. Well, it's nice of you to keep me posted about your activities—"

"Don't, Simon. Please don't." Rae hadn't realized that sarcasm delivered in a disinterested tone of voice could hurt so much. "I'm sorry for the things I said to you last night, but I don't think you have time to listen to my abject apology just now. Something else is much more important. While we were fishing, we came across a drifting rowboat miles from any speck of land."

"Empty?"

The question was quick, to the point, and painstakingly impersonal. "No," Rae replied, struggling to keep the information she was passing along equally devoid of emotion and completely factual. "An unconscious man was draped over one of the oars. The most incredible part of the whole thing was that he and Dr. Hamilton know each other. We've found the person there's been all the newspaper hoopla about."

"You're wonderful," Simon praised, forgetting for a moment that he was furious at her. "No names. Now—he's alive?"

"Yes. Very much so."

"Where?"

"Still aboard—aboard my friend's boat. You know the location of Dad's shop?"

"Yes. Norm and I will be there. Seven minutes."

They made it in six. Rae was delighted. It gave her sixty seconds less to dread the coming encounter. She was waiting at the head of the pier when a green sedan turned the corner.

Though neither border patrolman was in uniform, there was something about their stance, their watchful alertness, that marked them as officers of the law. Rae stood her ground during their quick approach, then turned and with a restrained hand gesture indicated the *Coral Belle.* Not a word was spoken until the three of them were aboard.

Simon stopped her then while Inspector Norm Peters identified himself and his partner to the group on deck. "Why did you call me? Why not the sheriff?"

"I didn't think it was his concern. Jeff and I talked it over and agreed that it was a problem for Immigration." Rae made herself look him in the eye. An expressive, brown, unblinking eye. "That's you—isn't it?"

"As near as makes no difference." Simon glanced to where his partner was assisting Manuel Villanova in the effort to sit up. "We could have had emergency equipment here if your Captain Carter had radioed ahead from out at sea."

"Where ambulances go, so do rubberneckers. Photographers too. Besides," Rae added, cut to the quick by his snide reference to *her* Captain Carter, "the *Coral Belle* isn't equipped with a powerful ship-to-shore hookup. I doubt Jeff's CB is effective for farther than a few miles."

"Well, it doesn't look as if the man is in that bad a shape, anyway," Simon observed. "If Norm and I support him between us, he'll likely be able to manage as far as the car."

She stood aside and let him do his work. Not that she had any choice in the matter. The movements of both officers were extremely efficient and allowed no leeway for personal discussions. Rae watched them assist the feeble refugee into the green sedan. To her surprise, though, there was only one border patrolman in the car when it drove away. Simon came striding back along the wharf in the direction of the large white cabin cruiser.

If she had expected him to be returning for a tête-à-tête, she was mistaken, however. By the time he swung aboard, Simon had a pen and notebook ready for a nitty-gritty question-and-answer session with all three of them.

"I didn't make any attempt to retrieve that rowboat, because by the time we got Villanova aboard the *Coral Belle,* the little boat I'd pulled him away from was surrounded by sharks," Jeff said pugnaciously when Simon returned to this point a second time. "If you'd like to try and corral it yourself, I can furnish you with the approximate latitude and longitude."

"That might be a good idea." Simon's pen poised over the page.

"Oh, for—" Though he'd never expected to be taken up on the offer, Jeff found himself furnishing the coordinates through clenched teeth.

Simon listened courteously to Dr. Hamilton's comments about their amazing discovery and had some penetrating questions about identification. "It was certainly fortunate for Señor Villanova that someone who knew him personally was aboard when he was found drifting around the ocean." Simon's voice was without inflection. "You're not gifted with ESP, are you?"

Cole Hamilton lifted an eyebrow. He hadn't dealt with students all those years without recognizing when he was being baited. "Only on Wednesdays," he replied evenly. "What I was gifted with today was a birthday celebration arranged by a very kind colleague and her friend. I assure you, we hadn't the least idea that we were going to find anything except fish out in that ocean."

The inquisition continued for another ten minutes. Rae found herself vacillating between admiration for Simon's thoroughness and exasperation with his seeming refusal to take anybody's word for anything. In response to one of the few questions any of them asked in return, they were informed that Manuel Villanova was already en route to a military hospital.

Simon's flat thanks for their cooperation left Rae with a feeling of anticlimax to a day that had already contained a little too much of everything. While Jeff made notes in his log and Dr. Hamilton got his fish out of the ice chest, Rae walked back to the railing with the man she had telephoned less than forty-five minutes earlier.

"Simon, about last night—"

His tone was no more encouraging than his expression. "I hope you enjoyed the rest of the dance."

Okay. I had that coming for the things I said to him. His feelings were hurt. Now he's hurting mine as a way of making sure the distance between us doesn't start closing again.

"Yes, thank you," Rae said evenly. Simon was right, she conceded. A cool, impersonal manner was the best method of handling things. Calm courtesy could get them both out of this no-win situation without loss of face on either side. "But naturally, I was curious about the outcome of that emergency call you received. Were you successful in finding your ferry-boat?"

"No, I'm afraid I'll be around Shell Bay a while longer, after all." There was nothing in Simon's dark gaze to indicate how he felt about that. "The boat that was spotted last night belonged to a couple of smugglers with more nerve than brains. The DEA has them and their contraband in custody."

Rae gave a little shrug and faked a laugh. "Win a few, lose a few, I guess."

"Oh, I don't know." Simon put a lean, tanned hand on the rail and hopped up onto the pier. "I'd say that last night was a dead loss all around."

About the only thing that changed in the next few weeks was the weather. With the winding down of August and the approach of fall, the hurricane season moved into high gear. Gradually the town emptied of all but its permanent residents. Come December, the tourists would be back in force; during the winter and early spring, "snowbirds" escaping the harsh Northern weather migrated to south Florida by every means of transportation. But at this time of year most of them counted themselves well out of it.

Inevitably, rumors drifted back to Rae, often through her father, who was acquainted with most of the area's merchants. Quiet questions were being asked about radio tubes. Casual, low-key visits were made without notice to charter boats. And from Brian came a stray bit of information: Coast Guard cutters on patrol had orders to pick up a derelict rowboat should they happen across it.

But if there was any suspicion concerning that boat, it did not seem to extend to Manuel Villanova. Following his recovery from his ordeal on the open sea and a confidential debriefing by federal agents who were deeply interested in everything concerning the island of Alta Monte since it had become the terrorist "Enclave," the scientist gratefully accepted the post that was offered him at the Avionics Lab.

"I didn't even recognize him," Rae murmured to Cole Hamilton as the two of them walked back to their offices following a staff meeting to welcome the new member of the team.

"Yes, that luxuriant toupee makes him look ten years younger," Dr. Hamilton agreed. "I don't think he's comfortable with it yet, though. Even in Emil Rausch's air-conditioned office, Manuel kept mopping his brow. He told me he never realized hair could be so warm. We thought he should wear it for his own protection, though, so he won't be recognized."

There was no doubt in anyone's mind that Project G.A.T.E. would benefit from the inclusion of Dr. Villanova into their ranks. He was particularly knowledgeable about the strengths and weaknesses of landing gear on jet aircraft and was able to suggest ways of reinforcing this critical area so that it would continue to operate even in the event of an on-board explosion.

Rae didn't think the scientist was very happy,

though, in spite of the fact that he had managed to escape from the Enclave and was doing the sort of work he liked best. Once an errand took her to the building's communications room. There she found him poring over international telephone directories. The slim volume in his hands listed exchanges on the island of Alta Monte, she noticed.

Manuel Villanova flushed a deep red when he realized that his interest in the book had been observed. "You will think me very foolish." He looked down at the page he'd been studying, then set the volume aside and pulled a handkerchief from his pocket to blot the moisture from his face.

Rae recalled a favorite old saying of her grandmother's: "Men sweat, ladies perspire." Whatever you called it, the moisture seemed almost to gush from this poor man's pores. She wondered if he would ever get used to the striking new hairpiece or if eventually he would be willing to risk his safety and return to being bald but comfortable.

"Why should I think of you as foolish?" she asked. "Anyone who's spent his whole life in one place is bound to be a little homesick for it, regardless of its drawbacks."

"You are very kind." A poignant smile touched the scientist's lips. "To tell the truth, I was trying to figure out some way to communicate with an old family friend back on the island. I wanted to beg him to . . . to make certain there were fresh flowers for my mother. For her grave, that is."

"I knew what you meant," Rae assured him.

"Well, I—I wish you success. I suppose mail coming in and out of Alta Monte is censored these days and phone calls monitored?"

"That is so." He cast a last longing look at the directory which was useless to him and turned away.

No, Rae thought again; he wasn't very happy. But then, neither was she. For weeks she had put off facing facts, but it was stupid to go on lying to herself. The problem was that she'd fallen in love with Simon Kirk, and there was absolutely nothing she could do about it except grit her teeth and try her best to put him out of her mind. He had never planned to stay on here. For all she knew, he was gone already.

It couldn't be too soon for her.

"I don't know, Dad." Rae shot an apprehensive glance at the peculiar gray sky overhead. "We've had several near misses this season already, but the meteorologists seem to think that Hurricane Jonathan is headed straight toward us. Are you sure your lodge members want to go ahead with plans for the picnic in spite of it all?"

"Of course I'm sure." With a stubborn look on his face Dan Travis climbed into the front seat of the light-blue Ford compact and fastened his seat belt. "That picnic's a tradition. Wait and see; they're going to downgrade Jonathan to tropical storm status any hour now."

"Oh, that's all, huh?" Her dad had the courage of his convictions, she'd say that for him. Rae put the car in gear and headed for the supermarket. With nothing else to do this long holiday weekend, she had volunteered to help with the preparations for the traditional Labor Day picnic he and his friends enjoyed so much. And it was quite true that nine times out of ten a storm that seemed to be headed straight toward their piece of coastline would veer off in another direction and wipe out Biloxi, Mississippi, or Cancun, Mexico, instead.

Besides, she told herself practically, even if they did get some heavy wind and rain, the lodge members could camp out in their meeting hall and congratulate themselves on not having let any old storm ruin their best annual treat. She could picture them now, roasting their hot dogs over the Jenn-Aire. It was going to be a challenge to work that softball game in, though.

The shopping cart was half full, and she was hunting for the barbecue sauce her father liked best when she spotted a familiar face a few yards down the aisle. "Hello, Alyssa." Rae gave a polite smile. "I see we're not the only ones planning a big feed for the holiday. Got some special Labor Day plans?"

"Weather permitting." Alyssa glanced at her own laden buggy and promptly changed the subject. "I haven't seen much of you at work lately, Rae. I guess that means the computer's been behaving itself, right?"

"So far," Rae answered. That was the simple truth, certainly. The darned thing hadn't had a chance to act up because for the last few weeks she had studiously avoided having anything to do with it. She hated being reminded that any day now the other members of the team were going to complete their phases of the research. Then the details of her "guardian angel" package would have to be programmed into that monstrosity.

But there was no point wasting a perfectly good holiday weekend worrying about her next encounter with a piece of machinery that almost growled every time she went near it. She'd deal with it when she had to. Maybe she could put the evil moment off until October.

Procrastination was not generally one of her failings. Ashamed at her cowardice where that blasted computer was concerned, Rae resolutely pushed these thoughts out of her mind and turned back to the shelf containing the barbecue sauce. In doing so, she saw that her father had already located the brand he preferred. He and Alyssa were having quite a discussion about the merits of the various flavors.

Where were her manners? Belatedly Rae performed introductions, noticing that her dad seemed to be unusually chatty. Though he enjoyed the company of people of all ages, he had seemed content enough with his status as widower these past few years. One of these days, though, she supposed he might get around to seriously looking for a new lifetime companion.

That was okay with her, she conceded, trying to view the matter unselfishly. Anyone—except Alyssa Fairfax!

It wasn't until they'd been through the checkout

line and were on their way home that Rae learned why her father had seemed so interested in the technician from the Avionics Lab.

"I hadn't realized you had so many foreigners working in that place," Dan Travis remarked.

Rae paused at a stop sign and looked over at him in surprise. "What are you talking about, Dad?"

"That Alyssa girl. I kept her gabbing as long as I could, in the hopes of putting my finger on that unusual quality in her voice, but darned if I could make it out."

"Well, I've noticed her being sharp-tongued on occasion, but I certainly would never have pegged Alyssa Fairfax as a foreigner," Rae demurred. "I think she must be from up North someplace."

Her father gave her a pitying look. "Honey, do you mean to sit there and imply that I wouldn't know a Down East twang if I heard it? Or the sort of palaver you'd get from an Ohio salesman, or a New Yawker"—he deliberately exaggerated the word—"or that funny way people from Massachusetts have of sticking in an extra 'r' here and there?"

"Well, no." A toot from the impatient driver behind her reminded Rae of where she was. She put her foot on the gas and got the car moving again. Another person making the sort of claims her dad just had might seem to be bragging, she mulled, but he was simply stating facts. He possessed an incredibly accurate ear for regional accents. Look at the way he'd pinpointed Simon Kirk's birthplace to the precise county and then picked up the fact that he had worked in the West before coming home to Florida. It was just a hobby with Dan Travis, but she really never *had* known him to misidentify someone's dialect or accent after having listened to them speak for only a minute or two. In phonetics he could probably give Professor Henry Higgins a run for his money.

"I'm sorry if it sounded as if I was doubting your word," Rae said now. "I was just kind of surprised, that's all. No one ever mentioned where Alyssa came from. Guess I simply took it for granted that she was native-born."

"Native-born somewhere, but not in this country," Dan Travis insisted. "Honey, did you remember to get an extra sack of cornmeal for the hush puppies?"

Chapter Seven

It bothered Rae.

For the rest of the weekend she found her father's assertion coming back to her again and again. Certainly, she thought, there was no hard-and-fast rule against foreigners being employed at the Avionics Lab. Look at Manuel Villanova, who'd been welcomed with open arms for his expertise in aeronautical design. And it was common knowledge that Dr. Emil Rausch, the lab's director, had been born in Germany. But he was just a small child when his Jewish family fled Europe to escape the growing Nazi power; the Rausches had been American citizens for decades.

Alyssa, though. . . . No one had ever raised the question of her nationality. Not until now, at least. And it certainly wouldn't be a good idea to go jumping to conclusions. Sure, her dad had a great ear where people's speech was concerned. But it was a hobby with him. Who in a position of authority was going to take the word of some amateur who ran a bait-and-tackle shop when it came to certifying where someone had come from?

They'd laugh at him. That's what would happen, all right. And Rae wasn't about to expose her dad to ridicule.

Still. . . . Well, it bothered her.

Throughout that threatening long weekend, while Jonathan yo-yoed from hurricane to tropical-storm status and back again, she brooded about the problem. To her vast relief and everyone else's the weather front backed off slightly in the middle of the night on Sunday and showed signs of blowing itself out down in the Gulf. They got the picnic in—just.

By Monday night the atmosphere was so still and hot and breathless, she almost wished it would cut loose—pour and get it over with. She hated having things hanging over her head.

Rae went to bed that night having resolved on a course of action. At the very first moment possible, she intended to take a discreet look at Alyssa Fairfax's personnel file. Perhaps that would settle the question, one way or another. If it listed the woman's place of birth as someplace outside these fifty states, she could come home and tell her father he'd been absolutely right. And if it didn't. . . .

Well, she'd cross that bridge when she came to it.

The storm had still not broken by the time she left for work on Tuesday morning. At the lab more than one person's nerves seemed to be under a strain because of it. Rather than having eased tensions, the three-day holiday appeared to have had an adverse effect on usually placid tempers. The Marine guard snapped a curt reply to Rae's cheery "Good morning," and even at eight A.M. the downstairs receptionist looked to be in a state of frazzled irritability.

"Good grief! Everyone around here seems to have turned into a grouch," she complained to Dana when she walked into her future sister-in-law's office fifteen minutes later.

"Oh, it's just the weather. A lot of people canceled the plans they'd made earlier, convinced that we were going to have a hurricane. Then when Jonathan failed to arrive on schedule, they figured they'd been cheated out of their holiday."

"Guess you're right. Speaking of holidays, how was yours?"

"Okay, considering Brian couldn't get any time off. He called twice, and we talked for hours." Dana turned on her word processor and got out a fresh shorthand book. "Since we're splitting the phone bills nowadays, I think I'd better get to work and earn my share. Was there something special you wanted, Rae?"

"Yes, actually there was." Busy herself, Rae appreciated Dana's efficiency. Her directness made it easier to state the request and be done with it. "I wondered if you'd run interference with Personnel for me. I want to look at one of their files without calling any attention to that fact. If I ask, they're going to wonder why, but—"

"But if the director wants every file in the place, they're his without question." Dana was well aware of her boss's clout. "Sure. Got your eye on that gorgeous hunk who works in Accounting, do you? Gonna check out if he's married?"

"Uh, not today." Rae didn't contradict Dana's assumption that a single woman of twenty-six would naturally be interested in someone as good-looking as Beau St. Giles, but just for a moment she had a flash of another face—a lean, tanned face with a solid, stubborn chin and velvety brown eyes.

She pushed away the memory of Simon Kirk and said, "Actually, it's Alyssa Fairfax's background I'd like to review."

Alyssa had once referred to Dana as a "dizzy blonde" in her hearing, a completely unjustified appellation. Dana grimaced. "Miss Efficiency been rattling your cage about botching up her precious computer again?"

"No, because I haven't touched the thing in weeks," Rae confessed. She knew the matter that had been troubling her must be reflected on her face. Aware that anything she told Dana would never go further than this office, Rae shared with her the concerns that had been niggling at her ever since that encounter in the grocery store Saturday morning.

Dana had often heard Dan Travis demonstrate his expertise with voices. Her mother was from Tarpon Springs, a town north of Tampa that was home to many old-timers of Mediterranean extraction who made their living diving for sponges. On a visit the Travis and Webb families had made there together to witness the blessing of the fleet, Rae's dad had unerringly picked out people born on Crete, Santorin, Mykonos, and Rhodes as well as identifying the accents of those from several areas on the Greek mainland itself.

"Your father's really good with voices." Even as Dana agreed, a note of reservation crept into her tone. "But—"

"But whether all these people with Ph.D.'s and high government positions would believe it could be done is another story," Rae finished for her. "You're reading my mind. However, the question will be academic if it turns out Alyssa spent her first five years in Portugal or some such place."

Dana decided it would be best to ask Personnel to send up the records on everyone from the Maintenance Department, rather than singling out the computer technician's file exclusively. "I can make some vague mention of a special job for Dr. Rausch needing to be taken care of soon and say we want to see whose qualifications might best suit the project."

A tactful approach was best, Rae agreed. The work they were doing here at the lab was vitally important, too essential to have anyone associated with the facility who wasn't exactly what he or she purported to be. On the other hand, if there was nothing to worry about, her superiors wouldn't thank her for needlessly raising suspicions.

"That sounds like a perfect way of handling it," she complimented Dana. "Give me a call when they arrive, and we can take a look together."

It was a relief to have done something positive in

the matter of tracking down Alyssa's roots. With the matter at least pushed to the back of her mind, Rae was able to buckle down to the work she'd been hired to do. She was just tucking away two new drawings pertaining to stress points in an aircraft's fuselage when her phone buzzed. Closing the wall safe, she bustled across the room to answer.

"Rae?" There was a guarded tone to Dana's voice. "Would you have a minute to stop in here on your way to lunch?"

"Sure. Be right there."

A very short time later she was scowling down at the page from the file Dana handed her and attempting to reconcile her own strong instincts with the information it contained. She might as well have attempted to convince herself that black was white.

"I don't believe it."

The expression on Dana's attractive face reflected the same opinion. "It hardly seems plausible to me, either," she said, "but these things are checked and double-checked for the security clearances all our employees must have. According to this, she has documentation stretching back to her first breath proving she was born in Charleston, South Carolina."

"I don't care what it says, that isn't true," Rae declared stubbornly. "Dad could never have missed on something like that. Besides, more than once I've done my darnedest to account for that antagonistic manner of hers by telling myself she wasn't brought up to be courteous and considerate like a Southern girl would be. But Charleston—why, if ever there was a bastion of the Old South, that's it! I don't care what sort of upbringing she might have had; a bag lady from Charleston could give Alyssa Fairfax pointers on gracious behavior."

"That's what I thought too," Dana agreed. "You know these hardheaded scientists we work with, though. They'd think we'd been working too hard if we came to them saying we had a hunch somebody might be fibbing about her hometown. And Security would poker up and demand to know what sort of proof we could furnish to challenge a government investigator's affidavit that this woman's background is above reproach."

"They'd be perfectly right in doing so too." Rae gave a somber nod. The days of the "Red Witch Hunts" were long gone, fortunately. Back in that Cold War era, many a reputation had been ruined by an unfounded allegation.

"But if there's even the tiniest chance that Alyssa isn't who she says she is—" Dana's apprehension was eased a bit by remembering the tight security preventing classified data from being smuggled out of the Avionics Lab. "Though I don't suppose that even that well-guarded gate is absolutely foolproof. If the terrorists were to learn the details of the work going on here, they might be able to find a way to circumvent it. Rae, how on earth are we going to handle this?"

"We can't. Not alone. We need help. The problem is, we can't talk about it to just anyone. Whoever we confide in is going to need a mighty high security clearance of his own. . . ."

Rae's voice trailed off. A lot of law-enforcement officers met that qualification. Particularly those engaged in undercover work connected with the nation's safety. The Border Patrol, for example. They waged a constant battle against infiltrators, drug runners, undesirable aliens. Also, that service was a branch of Immigration. They'd have access to the records of anyone entering the country.

For the past week or more, Rae had given up all hope of ever seeing Simon again. She had known from the very beginning that any sort of a future for the two of them wasn't in the cards. By now, in all likelihood, he had finished the investigation he'd been making along this stretch of the coast and been reassigned elsewhere. However, Shell Bay was a permanent base for Norm Peters. Talking to him wouldn't be like approaching a complete stranger, either, Rae told herself. They had met the day she and Jeff and Dr. Hamilton had found Manuel Villanova drifting around the Gulf after his escape from the Enclave.

She could give him a call and ask him in confidence if he would make a quick, quiet investigation into Alyssa's background.

"That's the only thing I can think of to do," she added in a worried tone after confiding the tentative plan to Dana. "Unless you've got a better idea?"

"No, I sure don't. Go for it!" She jotted down the most vital particulars from Alyssa's file and handed the slip of paper to Rae. "Inspector Peters will need a few dates and places to start with. I hope you can make him understand how important this is. It's going to bother me something fierce until it's resolved."

Rae glanced in the direction of Dr. Rausch's closed door. "You've got enough to worry about, just helping to keep things on an even keel here."

"That's true," Dana said with an earnest nod of her head. "Even without proof I think I'd share our concerns with the boss if it weren't for Project G.A.T.E. coming to a head practically any hour now. He got a phone call from an aide to the President this morning. Washington is getting anxious to start implementing the lab's recommendations."

"Then there isn't any time to waste." Rae started toward the door without further delay. "Go on to lunch without me, Dana. I'll join you in the cafeteria later on if I have a chance. The sooner Inspector Peters and I have a confidential chat, the sooner he can start looking into this matter for us."

As she slipped back down the hall, Rae could only cross her fingers that this plan wouldn't hit a snag. She tried not to think of what would happen if the officer refused to take her request seriously or attempted to downplay its importance. Simon wouldn't have done that, she knew. He might not have wanted anything more to do with her, but he respected her intelligence. He'd have known she wasn't the sort of person to go around crying wolf.

Her fears that Norm Peters might pooh-pooh the whole idea that a government employee might have falsified information to earn a security clearance was soon proved to be unwarranted. The first thing Inspector Peters asked was whether she was speaking from a secure phone. Since her office had just been swept for "bugs" that morning, Rae was able to reassure him on that point.

He listened in silence until she came to the suggestion that had raised her suspicions in the first place. "I know this is going to sound odd, but my father really is an expert with dialects and accents," she assured him earnestly. "It seems a little like tempting fate to ignore his insistence that the woman we're talking about wasn't born in this country."

"Travis," Peters repeated. "Would that be Dan Travis? The man who owns the shop down on the wharf?"

Here it comes, Rae thought. *He's going to ask how I expect him to take the word of some Florida Cracker who didn't even go to college over someone up in Washington with a clipboard and access to privileged information.* "Yes," she said, realizing her tone must sound defensive but unable to keep her temper from flaring. "Yes, that's my father. But if you think I'm exaggerating his ability—"

"I don't think any such thing, Miss Travis," Norm Peters said in a cool, even tone. "You're forgetting that I've spent the last eight years in Shell Bay. Your father's knack of telling where a person comes from by listening to him or her speak is darned near legendary around these parts. I certainly would be prepared to look into the matter on the strength of his word, even if there wasn't this connection with the Avionics Lab to take into account."

Rae's voice came close to trembling in relief. "Thank you, Inspector. I want to apologize for sounding a little edgy. I should have known you wouldn't form snap judgments. Please, could you check this out immediately?"

"If you could see my schedule, you wouldn't use words like 'immediately.' " It sounded as if he were only half joking. "What I can promise is to have this woman's background double-checked at the first possible moment. I'll get onto our own people in Charleston and ask them to give this question top priority. Now, I'll need the date of birth listed on her records and any other solid facts you can furnish."

By the time she hung up, Rae's morale had improved considerably. There was, she assured herself, a silver lining to every catastrophe. If she hadn't blown a tire and crashed into Simon Kirk's car—and through that incident gone on to learn more about the Border Patrol and form a high opinion of the agency's trustworthiness—she wouldn't have known who to turn to in this quest for confirmation of Alyssa's background.

It would have been a lot easier on her heart and soul, of course, if she could have arranged to cut out the middleman and simply have dealt with Inspector Peters from the very beginning.

Rae stood up, carefully folding the slip of paper containing facts and figures pertaining to Alyssa Fairfax and tucking it into her pocket. She'd return it to Dana to be shredded and incinerated with all the other sensitive materials at the end of the day.

Too bad she couldn't manage to get rid of unwanted feelings in the same way, she thought regretfully. And memories. Heart-tugging recollections of that "middleman" insisting he didn't get much time off. Then confessing that he wanted to spend hours, days, weeks in her company. And the most unwelcome memory of all—of him standing next to her on the *Coral Belle* and insisting that the evening they'd spent together had been a dead loss all around.

She pulled the office door shut behind her with a bang. In this life you didn't always get to make choices. Too bad. If that were possible, she'd have been able to put Simon Kirk out of her mind as easily as he'd dismissed her from his.

Right after dinner Dan Travis announced that it was time to do a little boarding up around the place. "We're likely to have a visit from Jonathan, after all," he added fatalistically.

Rae wouldn't have been a bit surprised if the hurricane had descended on them that very moment. The weather was miserable—hot and sticky, without a breath of air. And so quiet it was eerie. No bird calls and none of the usual little scurries of small creatures in the underbrush. Barefoot, she hurried back and forth across the kitchen vinyl, clearing the table while thinking ahead to emergency preparations.

"I rounded up spare flashlights and candles and the kerosene lamps days ago, so they'd be handy if and when we needed them," she said. "And if the power goes, there's plenty of stuff cooked to last us for days. Do you think this will be a bad one, Dad?"

He shot a somber glance out the window. The glowering sky was far darker than it should have been at that time of evening. "Hard to say, honey. Nothing about Jonathan has been predictable so far. But I'm kind of hoping Brian is safe in port 'stead of out on the cutter."

Rae hoped so, too, even though she doubted there was much chance of that. With a weather front this formidable approaching the Florida coast, the Coast Guard would be busier than ever.

Very seldom, in spite of the area where they lived, had Rae actually seen those two ominous square red flags with the black squares in their centers run up on the flagpole. A full-fledged hurricane warning was rare. Now she shivered, torn between wishing this beastly storm would get itself over and done with, and praying that it continued to hold off for the sake of anyone and anything that might lie in its path.

She had just filled several large containers with fresh water as a hedge against possible ruptured pipes when a sharp knock rose in competition to the rhythmic hammering coming from the rear of the house. Rae swung open the kitchen door, expecting to see one of her neighbors. Instead, the caller was a tall, lean man who didn't even live around these parts.

"Hello, Rae."

"Hello, Simon." The crinkles alongside his eyes had deepened, if anything, she noticed, but it honestly didn't look as though he'd smiled at all since the last time she'd seen him. "You'll have to forgive my surprise. I figured you had left town a long time ago."

"No, I've been here. Even busier than usual, of course."

"Of course." Rae brought her chin up another half inch. "I won't waste your time, keeping you talking. It was Dad you came to see, I imagine. Just follow the thuds of the hammer. He's boarding up the rear windows, getting ready for the big blow."

"Smart man. We've been put on alert too. But I didn't come to discuss the storm, and I'm not here to speak with your father, either," Simon declared. In spite of the fact that she hadn't asked him in, he stepped into the kitchen and firmly closed the door behind him. "I came to find out why you called Norm for help with a problem instead of me."

Rae folded her arms and continued to hover near the door. He'd be leaving soon, just as he always did, and she'd need to be handy to see him out. "Simon, I just told you that I was under the impression you'd left town. You made it very clear that your assignment here was temporary. I assumed that you'd finished the job you'd been sent here to do weeks ago and were working elsewhere nowadays."

A lock of dark brown hair fell across his brow as he shook his head. Impatiently Simon shoved it back. "No, the case I was assigned to investigate is still wide open. If anything, I've run into more questions than answers where a number of points are concerned."

"Oh, I'm sorry to hear that." Rae couldn't quite manage a smile to accompany the well-mannered response. "I wish you success in getting matters cleared up soon."

Simon glared down at her. That hard jaw of his bulged. He looked as though he wanted to grit his teeth. Maybe he was.

"You never let yourself get ruffled, do you, Rae? Nothing that happens is ever allowed to fluster you. You're always the courteous, calm, considerate Southern lady."

If only he knew, she thought. Just standing here next to him was like balancing on a bed of nails in her bare feet. Maybe it didn't show on the outside, but every time she congratulated herself on getting over Simon Kirk, all she had to do was picture him in her mind. At once that old familiar ache started up again, rasping like a dull file across her heart.

"I was brought up to be polite," she said quietly, hoping she wasn't going to spoil this totally unreal image he seemed to have of her by bursting into tears.

"Well, your folks did a darned good job." Simon's voice had a gritty abrasiveness to it. "Even when you're telling someone you can get along just fine without him, you sound as distant and cool as some royal princess. No kidding; you could give lessons in poise."

That tilted chin of hers started to wobble. She swallowed, hard. He didn't notice.

"Your control is really phenomenal," he went on in that hot, accusing tone. "I tried to take a page from your book. Last month I decided that no matter what it cost me, I was going to steer clear of you. But I—"

"What?" With uncharacteristic abruptness Rae broke in. "What do you mean, Simon—'No matter what it cost you'?"

"As if you didn't know," he snapped. "Try giving up everything I ever hoped to find. Try walking around day in and day out, seeing little snapshots of you in my head—"

"Why?"

There was a note of such sincere perplexity in her voice that it made Simon even angrier than he already was. "Why? I'll tell you why! Because in spite of my highly overrated common sense, I fell in love with you. The situation was absolutely hopeless, but do you think I could convince myself to drop it, let it alone? I just kept right on thinking that somehow there had to be a way we could make it work. But then you let me know in no uncertain terms that you couldn't care less what I chose to do, and—"

"I did no such thing!"

"I beg your pardon, that's exactly what you did," Simon icily contradicted her. "You told me to run along and do my thing, that you could get along just fine without me." With a scowl he took a step forward. His hard fingers curled around the soft, pale skin of her upper arms. Not gently, either. "What do you think you're doing, Rae, interrupting me every two seconds? Next thing you know, they're going to revoke your title as Miss Courtesy of Southwest Florida! Anyone would think I was actually starting to get under your skin—"

"Shut up, Simon!"

Rae had never used those words in her entire life. She didn't even notice the aggravated way they popped out. Once, just once, she wished she could forget every single thing she'd ever been taught about the way well-bred young ladies were supposed to behave. She wanted to knock this man down on the floor. Stomp on him. Stop him from making such terrible, untrue accusations.

"Just shut up, Simon Kirk," she growled again and settled for kissing him instead.

Chapter Eight

That was better. A whole lot better.

Snuggling into Simon's arms, Rae heard the thud of her heart competing with the hammer blows from the rear of the house. "Guess I told you," she remarked with a sheepish giggle. "Bet you thought I didn't know how to be that rude."

"Go ahead: Make my day!" Simon gave the words a twist of Clint Eastwood menace, then spoiled the effect by laughing in delight. "Come on; you're not finished yet, are you? Be rude to me some more."

"Nothing doing. Not until I let you know that I didn't mean what I said at the dance that night. At least not the part about finding someone else. But darn it, you had a job to do. I couldn't allow you to play the dutiful escort when every minute increased the danger—"

"Shut up," Simon growled. "The only thing I want to hear for the next half hour is you saying that you love me, Rae Travis."

Lifting her head, Rae fastened adoring green eyes on the man who'd been monopolizing her dreams day and night for most of the summer. "Simon, I love you with all my heart. For twenty-six years I've been waiting to find someone exactly like you. I never dreamed it would happen so fast, but it did."

"Music to my ears." He stroked her hair gently.

"But that doesn't solve our problems. What about your job? What about mine? How can we even get to know each other when—"

"Rachel!"

"Okay, I know that love is the most important thing. But I still don't see how we're going to manage—"

"What did I tell you?"

She shut up and kissed him some more.

By the time common sense returned, the sounds of hammering had ceased. Only their hearts continued to pound. Rae opened her eyes to meet Simon's earnest gaze. "We'll make it work?"

"We very definitely are going to make it work. But not, worse luck, starting quite tomorrow." He let out a sigh as he caught sight of the wall clock. Taking her hand, he led her over to the table. "Come on; sit down. I have an appointment at nine-thirty. Before I leave, I want to give you a rundown on what's turned up so far in connection with this Fairfax woman."

Sensibly Rae disengaged her fingers from his and walked over to the stove. "Go ahead; I'm listening. I'll pour us both some coffee while you talk."

"Well, first of all, the preliminary information that came through from our people in Charleston indicates that she is completely on the up-and-up." Simon reversed the wooden chair and sat, folding his arms over the rounded top of its back. "Don't scowl, honey chile. I'm giving you facts. The infant later christened Alyssa Marie Fairfax was born in Santee Hospital in Charleston, South Carolina, on the date you gave Norm over the phone. Her mother died of fever six months later. The little girl's father was a Navy commander. Since he was out to sea most of the time, he left her to be brought up by her grandmother."

Rae held her tongue, letting him talk. This, after all, was information she had requested, garnered by a professional investigator. Carrying the two mugs, she returned to the table and sat down opposite her love, taking in every word. She only wished these validated details of Alyssa Fairfax's early life rang true to her.

The child's widowed grandmother, a Mrs. Pembroke, owned one of the beautifully restored houses in Charleston's famed historic district. Alyssa attended private schools with extra outside lessons in ballet, French, and piano, then went on to a distinguished local college to complete her education.

It sounded like something out of a turn-of-the-century novel. "Is the grandmother still alive?"

"Unfortunately, no," Simon replied. "Both Mrs. Pembroke and Commander Fairfax died while Alyssa was in college."

"So Alyssa has no relatives who could identify her?"

"No, but it's likely that many of her former teachers and classmates could, if they were asked to do so," Simon pointed out reasonably. "Especially in their twenties, people change scarcely at all over a four- or five-year period. Right now our agents are in the process of getting hold of a yearbook from the college for the year Alyssa graduated. The photograph there can be compared with her passport picture taken a few months later—"

Rae perked up her ears. "Passport? She left the country?"

"According to a neighbor of the late Mrs. Pembroke, Alyssa decided to take a few months off for foreign travel after her graduation from college. Lots of people do that if they can scrape up the money," Simon added. "I spent several months in Mexico, polishing up my Spanish and getting to know and like the people down there. That experience was a tremendous help to me later on. You didn't go right to work after picking up your master's either, did you?"

"That wasn't because of a yen to travel," Rae told him. "My mother was very ill. I put my career on hold for a few months to spend all the time I could manage with her. As yet, I haven't been to Europe."

"Neither have I. But hundreds of thousands of American college students do go every year. Alyssa Fairfax was one of them."

"Oh, Simon, I'm not disputing her right to have done that. It would be a wonderful opportunity to see the Old World and all the things you've read and heard about all those years. It's just—"

"Just that her voice doesn't match her background." Simon's tone was neutral. He wasn't making any judgments one way or the other. "Now listen, Rae, I witnessed your dad's skill in pinpointing my own beginnings, and Norm insists he's an absolute expert where accents are concerned. He's human, just like the rest of us, though. Mistakes happen."

"Yes, I know. But it isn't only that!" Rae was beginning to feel a trifle desperate. "A little while ago you were mad because I behaved like a—what was it you said? 'A courteous, calm, considerate Southern lady.' That's how I was brought up to act. But, Simon, I was never given half the advantages Alyssa Fairfax had, growing up there on The Battery in Charleston, taking ballet and piano, having a special tutor for French, attending private schools. Yet regardless of that careful upbringing, not a bit of that privileged background is reflected in either Alyssa's speech or behavior. She's sharp-tongued and sarcastic; she goes around hurting other people's feelings; it's all she can do to be civil to Dr. Hamilton. Me she regards as an utter nitwit because for some reason that wretched computer and I don't get along."

He smiled. "Take my word for it, Rae. You aren't a nitwit."

"That's right; I'm not," she agreed heatedly. "I don't have ESP, either. But every instinct I possess is standing up screaming that that woman isn't who she says she is."

"One way or another, we're going to find out for sure," Simon assured her. "And while the investigation into her antecedents is going on, I'm making an effort to find out what she does with her spare time nowadays."

That afternoon, he said, he had changed into civilian clothes and dropped by Alyssa's current address, pretending to be looking for an apartment to rent.

"The landlady's a gossip. With only a little encouragement she started telling me all about her present tenants. Including Ms. Fairfax. Says she's about the quietest young person ever to take up residence in the complex. She's had the same studio apartment for the past year and a half. Doesn't smoke or drink. Never has visitors, male or female. Pays her rent on time and hasn't even got a parakeet."

"Sounds like a pretty dull life. Simon, *nobody's* that much of a goody-goody!" Rae had a sudden recollection of a laden shopping cart. "Alyssa had plans for the Labor Day weekend," she said, doing her best to picture the items in that buggy. "When Dad and I ran into her Saturday at the Winn-Dixie, she was buying a couple of thick T-bone steaks, corn on the cob, half a watermelon, and some great big juicy slicing tomatoes."

"Mmmm, my kind of picnic!"

"I think it must have been intended to be an outdoor feed," Rae said, confirming his judgment. "She remarked that she was going somewhere, 'weather permitting,' then changed the subject in a hurry."

"Too bad. The name of a boyfriend would have helped."

That was the sort of feast you'd feed to a man, Rae

acknowledged. "I don't believe she dates anyone from work. You know how gossip gets around. Alyssa is bright and competent and very good-looking," she added in a bend-over-backward attempt at fairness, "but not—"

"Not exactly popular. Well, the truth is bound to come out in time."

The word "time" spurred reactions from both of them. Simon shot a half-guilty glance at the clock. Intercepting the direction of his gaze, Rae felt the pressure of an approaching deadline.

"Look," she said, "please don't think I'm being unreasonable, but the truth of the matter is, there *isn't* a whole lot of time. Something—something at the lab is coming to a head."

When he waited expectantly, Rae bit her lip in distress. She was torn between the "need to know" imperative that draped a veil of secrecy over her professional endeavors and the necessity of impressing Simon with the importance of speed where this investigation was concerned. She was boxed in from every side. "Darn it! I can't tell you anything specific."

"There's no need to."

"Isn't there?" The green eyes had a look of deadly earnest now. Coppery freckles stood out like small exclamation points against her pale skin. "Do you have any idea of how vital this is? For the very first time the designs and recommendations of several scientists, engineers, and technical designers like myself are scheduled to be brought together into one composite schematic. If a printout of this data were to fall into the wrong hands—"

"Stall," he advised. "See that that doesn't happen."

"How? I'm only a cog in the wheel. One member of a whole team. Washington—the government wants something specific to work with before they start grounding aircraft and imposing modifications. Our director is being pressed hard for results."

There was no way Simon could miss the urgency in her tone. "That's why you're so worried about Alyssa Fairfax? All this innovative material will be entered into the computers she works with?"

He did understand, Rae realized, heaving a sigh of relief. He knew her concerns weren't just based on jealousy or dislike or something else that was petty in nature.

"Yes, that's it exactly! The computer is state-of-the-art. All sorts of safeguards and alarms are built right into it. Nothing can be retrieved without a series of passwords and entry codes that are kept smack up to the minute. And even if that were achieved, it seems impossible that the information could then be smuggled out of the lab. Our security is formidable.

"But, Simon, Alyssa is very, very good at what she does. And she's clever. Persistent. And aggressive too. I have a feeling she wouldn't allow *any*thing to stand in her way. If she *is*—well, someone else, and if in spite of all the security precautions she manages to get hold of those detailed specifications—"

He thought of the jumbo jet with the Hamilton

family and hundreds of other innocent, doomed passengers aboard. Of the Pan-Am plane that had gone down in Scotland. Of others—too many others. Crash by crash, explosion by explosion, the terrorists were making their ruthless influence on the world felt.

"Fingerprints might be the answer," he said thoughtfully. "I'm sure that's one of the things a strategic installation like the Avionics Lab would want to keep on hand for every one of its employees. I'll check with South Carolina, see if a thumbprint was required to get a driver's license back in the days Alyssa Fairfax was going to college there."

He scrubbed a hand across his thick-lashed eyes. For the first time Rae noticed how tired he looked. "Oh, Simon, how self-centered I've been! I've been pressing you to devote your full attention to my own concerns, without even asking you how your investigation is going. Has there been no success at all in finding that vessel you called the 'ferryboat'?"

"A question like that is asking to hear a whole spate of discouraging words." He grimaced and shook his head. "To be honest, I'm not much further along in that regard than I was the night you and Brian went looking for your alligator friend. Then, I was sure that shortwave message must have been meant to clue in a listening post on Alta Monte that a run was about to be made to smuggle one of their fanatics out of this country."

"You've changed your mind?"

"I was wrong about something," Simon admitted.

"Either there never was a fast boat engaged in that sort of activity at all, or it's operating out of some other area entirely, or—"

"Or you misinterpreted the meaning of that particular radio message that we interrupted," Rae concluded thoughtfully. "How about the other part of the search? That tube from a shortwave set I found was never traced?"

"Yes, I found out where that came from. Took a good bit of digging, let me tell you." After following dozens of leads that came to absolutely nothing, Simon went on, he had come across a small local firm specializing in estate auctions. "One of their employees recollected that a shortwave set had been part of the assets left behind by the former owner of a ship chandlery outfit when he died a couple years back."

"The man's possessions were all auctioned off?"

"By order of the distant relatives who'd inherited the estate. Such as it was," Simon added. "I gather there wasn't much of value. Old Mr. Farnham had been a ham-radio enthusiast for years. There was a lot of spare equipment with the set, according to the catalog they resurrected from their files, including assorted spare tubes. The set was so darned old that the manufacturer had gone out of business; they haven't made parts for it for at least the past fifteen years."

"I don't suppose the auction company kept a record of who bought what?" Rae asked hopefully.

"You optimist." Simon gave her a grin. He stretched, trying to ease the fatigue from his shoulders. Finishing his coffee, he untangled himself from the chair and reluctantly headed toward the door. "All sales were for cash, and not long afterward the auctioneer who handled the disposal of the Farnham estate moved out West to be near his grandchildren."

A thoughtful frown rumpled Rae's brow. "You mentioned that old Mr. Farnham had been a ship chandler. Doesn't it seem likely to you that he might have had a lot of supplies and various items among his possessions that might appeal to a seafarer?"

"Like someone with a good-sized cruiser, you mean? A boat with range enough to reach Alta Monte? That's exactly what I thought too. That's probably what attracted our unknown adversary to the estate sale in the first place. I don't doubt that the shortwave set was picked up along with all sorts of other odds and ends that would come in handy on a boat."

For more than an hour Rae had been so totally involved with Simon and the earnest discussion they'd been having that the approaching storm had gone clear out of her mind. Now, walking to the door with the man she loved, she saw that the wind had risen. The gumbo limbo tree that shaded part of the house was bent almost double.

Quickly she asked the last question that had been on her mind. Then, trying not to look worried, she kissed him good night and sent him out into the gusty darkness.

When the rosy glow of his car's taillights had faded from sight, Rae went back inside. Shivers caused by apprehension as well as by the whipping wind raced up her lightly clad body. Her father had come in through the front; she could hear the TV set rumbling in the living room. Pushing the kitchen door shut, she bolted it against the first ominous forerunners of Hurricane Jonathan.

Just before Simon's departure she had asked him about the date of the estate sale that had produced the shortwave radio. Now, walking over to the calendar taped to the side of the pantry door, she began checking back. Almost twenty months ago. Only weeks before Alyssa Fairfax had come to work at the Avionics Lab and moved into the complex where she'd been such an exemplary tenant!

Then her jubilation ebbed. Where was the connection? Alyssa didn't have a boat. Not even a pair of water skis, so far as she'd ever heard. Rae wondered if maybe she wasn't barking up the wrong tree, after all. At any rate, trying to link anything that happened so long ago with more recent events would take more time than she and the Border Patrol had to spare. She would just have to cross her fingers that other threads of the investigation would turn up the needed proof . . . before it was too late.

After more than a week of dillydallying around out in the Gulf, teasing and threatening every ship and sea gull and speck of land within a two-thousand-mile radius, Jonathan hit with a vengeance. Several times during that all but sleepless night Rae and her dad were up, checking rattling windows and doors, worrying about torn-off gutters, peering with concern at a damp patch on the ceiling.

Dan Travis aimed the rays of his powerful flashlight at the sodden plaster. "Must have lost a couple shingles off the roof," he concluded. "Probably be more gone before the night is over. Better get a pan under there before it starts leaking in earnest."

Rae darted off in search of something suitable, banging her shins on the low coffee table in the darkness. Judging by the inoperative clocks on their electric appliances, the power must have gone out somewhere around three-thirty. The water main might be next, she thought, very glad now that she'd taken the precaution the evening before of filling several large containers with drinking water. They'd be all right—she hoped.

By the time she returned to the living room with the pan, Mr. Travis had tuned his small, battery-operated radio to a twenty-four-hour news station. He was listening intently to estimates of wind velocity and details of damage reported up and down the coast.

It was pitch-black outside, shutting off any view of the Gulf. Trying not to picture tidal waves on the rampage, Rae asked whether people were being evacuated from their homes.

Her father shook his head. "Not here. Farther south, though. Late this afternoon they started getting everyone they could off the Keys."

That string of tiny islands was completely without protection from a big blow. The sandy, low-lying land could be inundated in a frighteningly short time. Rae knew that her dad must be thinking of Brian, just as she herself was, praying that a rescue attempt didn't turn into a disaster. Nor was her brother the only person on her mind that night. She was afraid for Simon, too, and for Norm Peters and the sheriff and his deputies who'd be out, doing their best to preserve lives and property. Every man and woman with a badge would have been pressed into service along the South Florida coast during this emergency.

At least they wouldn't need to worry about a "ferryboat" in weather like this, Rae thought, trying to see a silver lining. The most seaworthy vessel afloat wouldn't dare venture out just now. Not with winds currently being clocked in excess of one hundred miles per hour. Not unless it was responding to an SOS, at least.

But that would be the Coast Guard, she thought. The people connected with the boat Simon was looking for were far more likely to be taking lives than saving them. Terrorists didn't care who they killed or maimed, held hostage, or blackmailed into cooperating with them so long as their own fanatical goals were fulfilled.

Simon had made a mistaken deduction, he'd admitted earlier. Viewing the matter rationally, Rae found herself growing more and more convinced that it was in his interpretation of the message that he'd gone wrong.

That was certainly understandable. For months before that time, every signal that had been intercepted aimed at Alta Monte had followed an attempt at sabotage or some other act of terrorism along the Eastern Seaboard. Putting that together with other evidence, it had been logical to assume that those messages being beamed at the Enclave signaled the imminent return of an agent to that island. But this time there hadn't been a word in the papers to the effect that planes or airports were being menaced.

Which didn't mean that the same people hadn't sent that transmission. Just that on that particular occasion the content of it had been different.

With the wind howling like a demented banshee and buffeting the house with mighty, shuddering gusts, Rae knew she wasn't going to get much sleep, anyway. Lying there in the darkened room with the blankets pulled up to her ears, she went on wondering what sort of information could have been so urgent that someone would venture out into a swamp in the middle of the night to transmit the communiqué.

There wasn't a single answer she could think of that made any sense at all.

She finally did drift off, less than an hour before the alarm clock buzzed its imperative summons at the usual time. One glance outside, however, informed Rae that any attempt on her part to get to work that day would be utterly futile. Branches and other debris whipped through the air like tumbling fall leaves, propelled by gale-force winds. The crushed shell road branching off the main highway and running past the Travis home was blocked by uprooted trees and sections of somebody's picket fence. If the storm stayed on course, the eye of the hurricane was due to pass overhead late that afternoon. During that period of ominous calm Dan Travis hoped to climb up onto the roof and make some emergency repairs. After that they could look forward to the wind's renewed fury.

With the electricity out indefinitely, Rae rustled up a makeshift breakfast, feeding her dad store-bought Danish and hard-boiled eggs washed down with a glass of orange juice instead of the pancakes and grits and boiling hot coffee with which he usually started the day.

At eight o'clock she tried calling the lab. A recorded message informed her that the facility was closed for the duration of the storm. Employees were advised to stay indoors. The locations of several emergency shelters were given in case anyone's home suffered severe damage.

Well, it was an ill wind that blew nobody good, Rae thought, hanging up. With the lab closed, none of Project G.A.T.E.'s team would be there programming vital information into the computer. Every hour that step could be postponed gave the investigators probing into Alyssa Fairfax's background just that much more time to uncover the truth.

At noon, attempting to contact Dana to see if she had heard from Brian, Rae realized she had been lucky to get that call in to her office. The absence of a dial tone furnished silent testimony that their phone service had gone the way of the electricity.

Which meant that even if he had a moment free, Simon couldn't get in touch with her. She could only pray that he was safe and dry and well-fed . . . wherever he was.

In the early hours of Thursday afternoon, Jonathan's devastating winds and rains had moved farther east, to drench the cities of the Gold Coast and blow itself out, finally, in the Atlantic. The Travises had been luckier than some of their neighbors; the damage to their home was confined to torn-off shingles and the loss of a considerable amount of shrubbery. The Brannigans had been less fortunate: A falling tree had demolished their screened porch, and two windows on the west side of the house had been shattered by the wild gusts of wind.

Rae helped Mary collect the broken glass and sop up gallons of salty, fish-smelling water that the hurricane had left behind. Outside, her dad and Ed and several other neighbors toiled to haul away ripped-up planking from the porch and stack it in a corner of the yard until permanent repairs could be made. In spite of the property damage the general feeling was of relief. The hurricane was over, and none of them had been injured. Not everyone farther south had been that lucky.

Friday morning the usually placid Gulf was still gray and choppy, and the debris along the beach had to be seen to be believed. On the plus side, though, state troopers and workers from the Department of Highways had done a good job in clearing the roads and making them fit for careful use. As she started out from home, keeping both eyes open for possible hazards, Rae was torn between two outlooks. The sight of telephone-company trucks and busy linemen meant service would soon be restored. Simon and Brian would be able to communicate with the people they loved once again and trade assurances that everyone was safe.

On the other hand, if Jonathan had stuck around just a few hours longer, she and her colleagues would not have been expected to go in to work today. With the weekend coming up—well, that would have been an extra seventy-two hours to check into fingerprints and backgrounds and resolve her doubts one way or the other.

But she couldn't bring herself to be sorry the storm was over. The future held enough uncertainties as it was. She and Simon were in love; both of them knew now that this was the real thing. But they were also both committed to vitally important careers. Sooner or later Simon was going to be transferred. To somewhere in Florida, if they were lucky. Maybe as far away as El Paso, if they weren't.

But she couldn't go anyplace until her job was done. It might be a year, two years, even five, before the last of the drawings and recommendations were complete. What she and Cole Hamilton and Dr. Rausch and the others had been working on up until now was only the first wave, the preliminaries. The current studies were designed to reinforce and safeguard aircraft already in service. Next came an even bigger job. All future planes would feature a myriad of new design and flotation elements to render them capable of remaining intact even if a terrorist bomb should find its way aboard.

Rae thought about Dana and her brother, how they sometimes had months of separation between each meeting. If that's the way it had to be for her and Simon, that's the way it would be, Rae decided. She loved Simon Kirk. She wanted to be with him regardless of the sacrifices that might entail. Simon had told her they were going to make it work, and she believed him.

It had to!

Rae put these worries aside as she pulled into the lab's parking lot and steered the little Ford carefully around palm fronds and other obstacles deposited on the asphalt by the storm. Already gardeners had made progress in clearing away the debris, though, and she noticed the optimistic expressions on everyone's faces as they swept. It was as though Hurricane Jonathan had cleared the air, given them all the incentive to work toward a tomorrow that was bound to be better.

The Marine guards, the gate security people, and even the efficient young receptionist down in the lobby seemed to reinforce this outlook. There was a buzz of excitement going through the building, affecting even the elevator operator. Maybe it was relief at having survived the storm, Rae decided.

But the moment she stepped out onto the polished, third-floor corridor, she knew it was more than that.

Already in his long white lab coat, Dr. Hamilton was on his way back from the director's office with a file folder clamped under his arm. He paused before entering the room next to hers and gave her a smile of genuine welcome.

"Great to see you again, Rae. I imagine you're as excited as the rest of us. Now that the storm's over, we can really get busy."

"Excited?" Rae shrugged out of her jacket and gave her colleague a bewildered look. "Is there something special going on that I don't know about?"

"I thought you would have gotten the word," Cole Hamilton said impatiently. "Everything's all set. Today's the day. Emil Rausch wants the entire program entered into the computer by noon!"

Chapter Nine

Ten to one Rae was going to lose her job.

She faced that fact as she entered the last increments of data into the computer and slumped wearily back in the chair at her workstation. The buff manila folder containing the pages she'd copied from gave mute testimony to the awful step she had just taken. Dated more than a year ago, it was labeled: *Initial Stress-Support Diagrams. Proven Counterproductive. DISCARD.*

The graphics on which the computer entry she'd just finished were based were the very first designs she'd experimented with after coming to work here at the Avionics Lab. A great deal had been learned from those trial-and-error schematics. The early mistakes had shown her options to avoid and pointed to more beneficial strategies in reaching her goal.

These preliminary drawings not only contributed exactly nothing to the Project G.A.T.E. package. By programming this misleading information into the computer, Rae was well aware that she had completely invalidated the input furnished by the rest of the team. The resulting mishmash would be of no earthly use to anyone, whether as a resource in reinforcing a jet aircraft or in seeking stress points to sabotage.

Not that the time spent developing the painstaking program would be lost. Dr. Hamilton and the others could easily duplicate the data by consulting their files. With the addition of her "guardian angel" package, still safely locked in her wall safe, the program would be ready for use.

Still, the inevitable delay was going to cause a great deal of ire unless Rae missed her guess. Here and in Washington. And on Alta Monte too? She didn't know. All she could do was hope.

Had there been one hint, one concrete shred of evidence in the information Simon had passed on to her Tuesday evening that the computer technician was an imposter, Rae would have taken her courage in hand and argued for a delay in committing anything to the computer. But facts were one thing and gut instinct something else entirely. As much as her common sense and excellent work were respected here at the lab, Rae knew that without proof she could never have convinced the director to postpone the program. Not with a Senate committee breathing down his neck and the FAA clamoring for results.

So instead of making a fool of herself, she had simply listened to her conscience and gone along with Simon's advice to stall.

Rae straightened up and scooted her chair in a little closer as she prepared to add her name and employee number to the gobbledygook she'd spent the morning entering into the computer. This was going to stall the project, all right, she told herself. Not to mention putting her career in reverse!

It was a shock to place her fingers on the keys with no results. Unusually cooperative for the past few hours, the keyboard had suddenly become unyielding. Rae glanced in disbelief at the display screen with its winking cursor. Everything she'd entered so far was still intact. But it seemed this monster was determined to allow not another symbol into its memory banks until an expert with a deft touch adjusted its innards.

"I wonder. . . ."

The coincidence of a breakdown at this exact moment was too obvious to be disregarded. As Rae stared at the recalcitrant terminal, her suspicions that certain events were being carefully orchestrated deepened still further. For months the delicate microchips and electronic linkages had behaved beautifully—for everyone except her. It was almost as if someone had *wanted* this particular unit to keep breaking down so that when it happened at a critical moment, it would be just another instance of poor, fumble-fingered Rae Travis not getting along with the computer.

A glance at her watch told her that by now the other members of the Project G.A.T.E. team would have finished entering their findings and recommendations via the terminals in their own offices. Her input was to have completed the study, tied it all together.

It was too much to believe that the computer had chosen this exact moment to go kaput by accident.

So now what? Play along with them? She'd botched up the program so thoroughly that neither friend nor foe could benefit from it. The limb she was out on was already mighty shaky. She couldn't go back now. Might as well see this charade through to the end.

Half an hour later, struck by an eerie sense of déjà vu, she watched Alyssa prepare to delve into the depths of that space-age mechanical marvel. For once she felt no sense of guilt at having, somehow, gummed up the works. This wasn't due to anything she'd done, Rae assured herself. As sure as she was standing here, she knew that Alyssa had planned this moment to the split second. Right down to the seemingly random occurrence of allowing a tiny round piece of metal to slip from her fingers and bounce off across the floor.

"Oh, good grief! Catch that thing! Don't let it get lost."

Responding to the urgency in Alyssa's voice, Rae leaped to retrieve the rolling object. Her back was turned toward the computer for no more than a second, two at the most. It seemed impossible that the woman seated in front of the keyboard could have accomplished whatever it was she had come to do in that brief a time. Yet as she swiveled around and straightened up, Rae caught a flash of triumph in those glittery dark eyes.

Nothing seemed out of place. Alyssa's hands were

empty. Rae's gaze probed the long, full sleeves of the woman's striking red blouse, noting the fact that they were elasticized at the cuffs. An item could have been pushed up inside one of them in less time than it took to think about it.

"You really should be more careful," Rae said deliberately, handing back the tiny bolt that had created the diversion. "You never know when something important is going to get lost."

Alyssa looked as if she wanted to laugh out loud. "I'll remember that," she said, dropping her eyes back to the swirl of colored wires to hide her expression. In record time she had the machine reassembled and was out the door.

As the door latched behind her, Rae stared down at the computer. She would have been willing to bet a month's salary that its days of preprogrammed breakdowns were over. Alyssa didn't need it anymore. She'd been setting this up for a long, long time, and now she had won. So she believed, at least. But, Rae reminded herself, if a way weren't found to prove that Alyssa had helped herself to classified material, that bet involving the month's salary was due to be academic.

Unless one counted severance pay.

Shortly afterward, abashed at the thought of facing any of her colleagues after having sabotaged their joint effort, Rae decided to see what the vending machines at the end of the hall had to offer, rather than going down to the cafeteria for lunch. She was just heading back to her office with a can of diet lemon-lime in one hand and an apple in the other when a sharp harangue made her stop in her tracks. The scathing tones were coming from the communications room, where the door had been left slightly ajar.

"It's taken me twenty minutes to track you down," Alyssa Fairfax snapped angrily. "What are you doing in here?"

The icy can of soda she was holding sent little shivers up Rae's arm. But it wasn't half as cold as that insulting tone. She took a step closer to the unlatched door, wondering who on earth the woman could be speaking to. To her distress, the low-voiced reply was completely inaudible.

"That had better be the only reason." There was real menace in Alyssa's tones, as though she knew herself to be quite capable of carrying out any threat she made. "I've gone through a great deal to get my hands on this item, and no one's going to stand in my way of getting it out of here. Take it. You know what to do with it. And you know what will happen if you don't follow the rest of your instructions exactly as specified."

Clearly Alyssa had the upper hand over the other person in that room. Rae jumped as the abusive tirade increased in volume. Alyssa was only a few feet away from that door. Any second now she would come bursting out into the hall. Who knew what desperate steps the woman would take if she realized part of her plans had been overheard?

Trying not to picture a hostage situation with herself in the middle of it, Rae decided that, for a moment or two, discretion was the better part of valor. The ladies' room was two doors down on the opposite side of the hall. She could scoot in there, then hurry out to confront Alyssa's unwilling confederate as soon as the other woman had gone.

It was obvious to her that the other person was being bullied or blackmailed into cooperating. Maybe whoever had been behind that almost-closed door with Alyssa could be persuaded to help turn the tables on that woman.

If not, at least she'd know who to warn the gate guards to watch. The security precautions were up to the minute; it didn't seem possible that anything could be smuggled out. Yet Alyssa's confidence had never wavered. To be forewarned was to have the jump on her, Rae decided.

But thirty seconds later the communications room was empty not only of Alyssa Fairfax but of her cohort as well.

Rae spent the next three hours writing up a report to explain exactly what she had done that morning and why. She emphasized the fact that the guardian angel package she'd worked out so painstakingly was locked intact in her wall safe. The other members of the team would need only to enter their own research data into the computer, then add her program in its correct sequence. The result would be the first phase of Project G.A.T.E., ready for implementation.

Sealing the typewritten sheets in an envelope, she carried it next door to Dr. Hamilton's office. It was her intention to ask him to turn it over to Dr. Rausch first thing Monday morning. By that time, she thought fatalistically, Simon's contacts would have had the chance to check and confirm every detail of Alyssa Fairfax's life. She would either have the proof needed to back up the action she had taken—or be prepared to pay the penalty for her rash decision.

For once Cole Hamilton appeared to be completely relaxed. The tension had been lifted, at least temporarily, with this phase of the vital research program wrapped up. Rae was delighted to hear the lighthearted way he and Manuel Villanova were discussing the possibility of a weekend jaunt to unwind from the stress of the pressure they'd been under.

"I doubt this would be a very good time to go down to the Keys," the man from Alta Monte stated. "It's going to take them weeks to finish mopping up after Hurricane Jonathan down there. The roads are still hazardous right now too. How about a shelling expedition to someplace nearby instead?"

Both Rae and her colleague were well aware of Señor Villanova's expertise in this field. The enthusiastic amateur conchologist seemed to spend every spare moment combing the beaches for washed-in treasures. He knew the Latin names for the shells Rae had always referred to as banded tulips and lettered olives and rams' horns. One morning he had come in with a beautiful spotted Junonia to display to the others at the lab.

"I've always heard that right after a storm is the

best time to go shelling," she said now to Dr. Hamilton.

"Absolutely." Manuel Villanova nodded his agreement. "Shells from all over the Caribbean will have been washed up on the beaches as a result of the winds and unusually high tides. There's a sandbar not far south of here that several people have mentioned as the ideal spot for shelling. Why don't the two of us go investigate it tomorrow? I guarantee there'll be some rare specimens."

Dr. Hamilton laughed and said that perhaps it was time he became interested in a new hobby. "I haven't done much playing these past few years, I'll admit. All right, it's a deal! Why don't I drop by the motel where you're staying and pick you up at seven tomorrow morning?"

An odd expression crossed Manuel Villanova's face as he stood up and agreed to the arrangement. Before Rae had a chance to try and decipher it, a large white handkerchief was in the way, dabbing at the beads of perspiration on his brow. He didn't seem to have grown any more accustomed to that toupee in the last month, she thought, feeling sorry for him. He probably hated the disguise.

"I certainly hope the two of you have a marvelous outing." Rae hesitated a bit longer, hoping Villanova would leave so she could make her request in private. When he showed no signs of doing so, she had no choice except to go ahead and ask her favor with him still in the room. She handed over the envelope containing the report she'd written. One day would it be viewed as a confession?

"First thing Monday morning, would you mind delivering this to Dr. Rausch?"

"Certainly, if you want me to." Cole Hamilton looked rather uneasy at the prospect. "Rae, this isn't anything that's going to distress us all, is it? You aren't resigning your position, are you? Or eloping over the weekend?"

"No, neither one." She had no desire to quit her job, but Rae would have given a great deal to be able to answer the second part of his question in the affirmative. How wonderful, she thought longingly, if she and Simon could do exactly that. It wouldn't matter where they went so long as they were together—with no concerns about cruisers on clandestine missions, eerie radio signals, or masquerading technicians hanging over their heads.

But it wasn't in the cards. Not yet.

"My dad would never forgive me if I ran off and got married," she added, managing a faint smile to go along with her light response. "He's been looking forward for years to giving me away himself. There *is* a possibility that I might be a little bit late on Monday. I'd appreciate your helping me out this way."

"Consider it done."

Hard on the heels of Dr. Hamilton's agreement, Manuel Villanova broke in apologetically. "If you will excuse me, there is something I have neglected to do," he said, tucking the handkerchief back into his pocket and turning toward the door. "Until tomorrow morning, then."

Fearful that Dr. Hamilton would come up with a few more awkward questions to ask if she were there for him to quiz, Rae took advantage of Villanova's departure to make a quick exit of her own.

She collected her things from her own office, then waited her turn to be cleared through the security gate. For more than an hour afterward she waited in her car, watching the employees of the Avionics Lab leave. One by one they passed through that seeing-eye gate. At any moment she expected to see the guards sound the alarm, confiscate classified material, make a prompt arrest. But to her bewilderment the Friday-afternoon exodus straggled along as uneventfully as ever.

Rae headed home feeling as if the weight of the world were pressing down on her shoulders. With her own ears she had heard Alyssa admit having taken great risks to get her hands on something. Behind that almost closed door of the communications room she had passed the contraband on to her confederate. And somehow—*somehow*—that other person had managed to spirit it through the gate without being detected.

It was hard not to blame herself, to reason that she could have done more to prevent such a treasonous thing from happening. But in her heart Rae knew that no one would have believed her even if she had spoken up. Alyssa had been planning this coup for months. She'd have laughed in Rae's face and challenged her to prove that she'd done one thing wrong.

And she couldn't, of course. It was infuriating!

Phone service had been restored. The instant she reached her house, Rae tried putting a call through to Simon.

"I'm so sorry, my dear," Mrs. Peters replied when Rae had identified herself. "You've only just missed them. Simon tried half a dozen times to reach you before they left. I know there was some information he was very anxious to pass on to you."

And her fruitless vigil outside the gate had prevented him from doing so! Rae muffled a groan. "Do you know when he might be back?"

"Wish I did," Jessie Peters said regretfully. "They were headed up to Port Charlotte, below Sarasota, and I understand there's a bridge out that makes it slow going up the Tamiami Trail. Norman warned me not to look for them back tonight."

"Port Charlotte!" Rae exclaimed. "Isn't that out of their territory?"

"Well, yes and no. I gather this trek has to do with a boat that's been very much sought after. But I really don't have any definite information," Mrs. Peters quickly added.

She didn't need any more definite information than that, Rae thought, courteously thanking Mrs. Peters and leaving a message for Simon to call her as soon as he returned, regardless of the time. The ferryboat had surfaced at last!

It was hard to decide whether to be thankful or depressed at the news. Having the boat suspected of ferrying the terrorists back and forth to Alta Monte finally show up meant that Simon would be able to bring his assignment to a successful conclusion. It also meant that his transfer would be coming up any day.

The only silver lining she could think of was that if she got fired, she'd be able to move closer to wherever he was assigned. But she didn't want to give up her vital career, and especially didn't want to leave the lab under a cloud.

That was exactly what was going to happen, though, if she couldn't prove that Alyssa Fairfax was some sort of agent bent on securing the findings of Project G.A.T.E. for reasons of her own.

What little sleep Rae got that night was filled with worries and dreams—no, nightmares. Each time sheer exhaustion forced her eyes closed, she'd find herself tumbling into a world inhabited by shadowy conspirators and speeding boats and Marine guards with fixed bayonets challenging her about the awful thing she'd done to the computer program.

The shrilling phone on the bedside table awoke her shortly before eight. Rae sat bolt upright, grabbing for the instrument, whispering a prayer of thanksgiving that Simon was back at last.

But the caller wasn't Simon. Instead, Rae was astonished to hear Dr. Rausch asking if she knew anything about Cole Hamilton's present whereabouts. His abrupt tone was enough to yank her out of grogginess even more fully than a cold shower could have done.

"As far as I know, he and Manuel Villanova planned to go shelling today," she replied. "I was in Dr. Hamilton's office yesterday when he arranged to pick up Señor Villanova at around seven."

"An hour! A whole hour's head start!"

The exclamation didn't seem to have been meant for Rae's ears. Tersely Dr. Rausch asked if she had any specific information regarding the location of this shelling bed.

"No." Rae's worry increased with every word he said. It was Saturday! What in the world could have happened that he'd be seeking Dr. Hamilton so urgently? "Señor Villanova did say something about sandbars," she went on. "But you know shellers—they're pretty close-mouthed about where the really good specimens can be found. Is—is something the matter?"

"Yes, I'm afraid so," Dr. Rausch said heavily. "I came into the office this morning to catch up on some paperwork I've been shunting aside with this heavy concentration on Project G.A.T.E. There was a letter from Manuel Villanova pushed underneath my door. Evidently he had not expected me to find it until Monday."

Rae had a sudden vision of herself handing an envelope to Dr. Hamilton. Almost immediately Manuel Villanova had declared there was something he'd neglected to do. Had it been her own report that had given him the idea to communicate with the director?

"This letter," she prodded. "It concerns Dr. Hamilton?"

There was such a lengthy pause, for a moment Rae feared the connection had been broken. "This is hardly a matter to be discussed over the telephone," Dr. Rausch said at last. "But, yes—a concern has arisen regarding Cole's safety. If by any chance you should remember further details of yesterday's conversation, you are to get in touch with me immediately. Is that clear?"

"Yes, sir. I'll do that."

Six minutes later Rae was in her car on her way down to her father's shop on the wharf. She had taken time only to brush her teeth, splash water on her face, and drag on a tank top and a pair of cutoffs. Snatching up hairbrush and sandals, she had grabbed her car keys and headed for the driveway.

Mr. Travis and his neighboring merchants had teamed together to spruce up the wharf area following the gale winds and heavy seas that had accompanied Hurricane Jonathan. Rae found her dad using hammer and nails to replace a couple of planks that had been ripped loose from the pier.

"Dad, you know everything about fishing and shelling that goes on around here," she said, dropping down beside him. "Have any of your customers ever told you about a sandbar south of here that's likely to be the best place to collect shells after a big blow?"

He sat back on his heels, his forehead rumpled in thought. "Leroy Hibbings picked up a pair of pretty fancy Chinese Golds last season," he said. "He didn't want the location noised around, but he was pretty proud of that find. Told me there was a big hooking sandbar down below Gull Point a mile or so. Forms a natural net for things washing in when the wind is just right."

"Yeah! Come to think of it, I've heard about that place from a couple of others too. That must be the spot Señor Villanova meant."

There wasn't time to explain. Rae wasn't exactly sure herself what was going on, but instinct warned her not to waste precious minutes dissecting events at a time like this.

"Dad, I need to take a run down there. Is it okay to borrow your motorboat?"

"It is *not* okay." There was no compromise in Dan Travis's firm tone. "The water's full of debris from the storm. All the way over here this morning, I was dodging logs and uprooted mangroves, and heaven knows how much other flotsam and jetsam. What do you want to go down to that sandbar for, anyway? I thought you'd gotten over your seashell mania years ago."

"That's true, but I have a hunch that's where a couple of my colleagues were headed this morning. Dr. Rausch called a little while ago and mentioned that one of them might be in trouble." Rae put her hand on her dad's arm, earnestly assuring him that the errand she meant to undertake was no mere whim. "As soon as I go, I want you to call the lab and ask for the director. Tell him exactly what you told me—about that sandbar south of Gull Point."

"I'll be glad to make the call, but you still don't have permission to take the motorboat." Mr. Travis looked over at the marina a hundred yards up the shoreline and pointed to a familiar-looking cabin cruiser. "There's the *Coral Belle,* taking on a load of fuel. Get Jeff to run you down to where you want to go. He was just complaining to me the other day that he wasn't getting to see enough of you recently."

Rae knew that her father wasn't an alarmist. If he insisted that it was unsafe for her to undertake a several-mile trip in a small motorboat, then he was probably right. Besides, she could make a lot better time aboard the cruiser, anyway. And if Dr. Hamilton was sick or something, Jeff could help her bring him back.

She still didn't understand why Manuel Villanova should have slipped a letter under Dr. Rausch's office door or why the information it contained should have made the usually unflappable director moan things to the effect that they already had an hour's head start. But that could all be worked out later. Right now the important thing was to find the men and bring them back so that everything could be cleared up.

"Okay, Dad," she said, hopping up off the well-worn planks. "I'll impose on Jeff's good nature. Please run and get hold of Dr. Rausch right away, will you?"

* * *

Minutes later Rae got hold of Jeff and made her request.

"Sorry." Jeff shook his head. "No can do. I've got a charter party waiting. We're heading out to the Bahamas just as soon as I get the rest of the supplies aboard. I'll take you shelling next week, okay?"

"Jeff, I don't want to go shelling. Dr. Hamilton and that fellow we rescued out in the Gulf the day of his birthday party have taken off for some sandbar a few miles south of here, and I need to bring them back in a hurry. It's important."

"Why?"

She could hardly blame him for sounding so dubious. "I don't know exactly, Jeff; I just know that it is. Dr. Rausch, the director of the lab, phoned me half an hour ago, trying to locate Dr. Hamilton. Something urgent has come up at work, I guess."

"Something urgent's come up at work for me too," he said. "It's called making a living. I'd like to help you out, Rae, but I'm afraid it's impossible this time."

"Okay. I guess I understand." Rae started to turn away from the pilings to which the big cruiser was moored. "You have a good trip now. That looks like one of the sheriff's cars down the way. I'll have the deputy run me down. Probably be faster by road, anyway."

"No!" A thunderous scowl fulminated across Jeff's face. "Those poor guys are asleep on their feet, what with the hours they've been putting in the last few days." He stepped back from the railing. "Hop aboard, Rae. I'll help you find your friend."

"Thanks, Jeff. I sure appreciate it."

She waited while he handed a wad of bills to the dock attendant to pay for the fuel, then she untied the painter and swung herself onto the deck.

A minute later the powerful twin engines roared. The wharf slipped away behind them. As the *Coral Belle* headed out into the Gulf, Rae kept her eyes fixed anxiously ahead, on the alert for signs of a hooking sandbar.

Chapter Ten

Civilization ended about a mile below Shell Bay. That's the way it appeared from out in the Gulf, at any rate. Beaches were gobbled up as twisted dark mangroves pushed their gnarled roots shoreward out of the swamps. Here and there the black, oily coil of a small river squirmed inland, to disappear into the dense interior of the Glades. This was a Florida tourists seldom saw, Rae thought. A primitive, forbidding land as far removed from Disney World and the Kennedy Space Center as its modern-day citizens were from the Spaniard Ponce de Leon, who stepped ashore in 1513 to search for the Fountain of Youth.

"Gull Point." Jeff pointed to a spit of land jutting out from shore.

Rae lowered the binoculars she'd been using to scan the coastline. Now she focused instead on the nautical chart spread out in front of them. Depths were marked in fathoms at regular intervals; buoys pinpointed; hazards to navigation identified. She indicated a fishhook-shaped curl of land shown lying offshore a short distance south of their present position.

No doubt about it, the shelling there would be fantastic. But the sandbar appeared to be inaccessible without a boat.

Jeff monitored the depth-finder as the *Coral Belle* eased closer to the low-lying bar, more than a little concerned about running aground. "One sandbar, no shellers," he announced in satisfaction. "See—I told you this was a wild-goose chase. Let's head back."

Stubbornly Rae shook her head. "Please, Jeff, just a little farther! This is the sandbar Dad was telling me about, but I doubt that my friends realized they'd need a boat to reach it. Less than a mile on down the coast is another likely spot, though." She eased her finger along the chart. "Look. This beach would be accessible from shore, and the road doesn't lie very far inland at this point, either."

"Ah, look, Rae, this is a big waste of time. Yours *and* mine," Jeff argued. "If I don't get back pretty soon, I'm going to lose a mighty lucrative charter."

Ordinarily Rae's deeply ingrained consideration for other people would have caused her to bow to his wishes. He'd already done her a huge favor in bringing her this far. But Dr. Rausch had sounded so upset this morning that even now fear clutched her heart as she thought of what might have happened to Cole Hamilton. How Manuel Villanova fit into all this, she didn't know, but recent events had taught her all too well that unscrupulous people who would stop at nothing to achieve their ends didn't exist only in books and movies.

"The *Coral Belle* is so speedy, she can do another

few miles in less time than it takes to bicker about it. Please, Jeff. An extra twenty minutes is all I'm asking for. If we've still found no sign of them after that, you can take me back to the wharf, and I'll round up a small posse to help me press the search by land."

The grave look in Rae's green eyes told Jeff just how serious she was about this quest. In disgruntlement he veered around the sandbar and once again pushed the throttle forward. Rae picked up the binoculars to continue scanning the coastline off their port bow. Disappointment crowded in on her as the cabin cruiser plowed a frothy wake through the Gulf. There was driftwood and other storm debris aplenty all along the shore here, and flocks of birds everywhere. But not a sign of a human being.

Suddenly, then, a curve of beach jutted out, and Rae was pointing in excitement. "Jeff, look! Fresh footprints just above the high-tide mark!"

Jeff's set expression tightened. Clearly he distrusted whatever it was he suspected they might find. Swinging wide to avoid a bobbing log, he nosed the *Coral Belle* as near to the shallow cove as he dared before releasing the barbed weight of the anchor. Then he picked up the binoculars she'd been using and zeroed them in on the shore.

"Not a soul," he announced. "Zilch. If your friends were ever here, they've come and gone."

"Maybe not." Rae leaned against the rail, shading her eyes, wishing she could penetrate the thick foliage. "They might have decided to take time out and walk back to Dr. Hamilton's mini motor home for a bite of breakfast. It can't be more than a few hundred yards out to the road. It would be stupid not to see this all the way through after having come so far."

"Nobody would ever call you stupid. Just persistent as the devil." Jeff gave her an exasperated look and chucked a rope ladder over the side. "If it'll make you feel better, I'll swim ashore and take a check around."

Rae bent to slip off her sandals. "I'll come too."

"Nothing doing." There wasn't a hint of compromise in his tone as Jeff retrieved the pistol he kept up in the cockpit, checked to be sure it was loaded, then shoved it into a waterproof pouch. "Snakes," he explained succinctly, seeing her startled look. "Maybe gators as well. You don't want to go walking in on something you can't handle, hear me?"

There was an odd, rough note to his voice, one she had never heard before. During the many months she had known him, Rae had grown accustomed to Jeff's halfhearted flirtatiousness. She had a hunch that he was far fonder of the *Coral Belle* than he ever would be of any woman. But just then it had sounded as if he really cared about her safety.

The notion touched her heart. "Okay," she agreed. "Watch out for yourself, Jeff. And if you find my friends—"

"I'll tell 'em to take their seashells and run along home. Stay here!"

Without waiting for an argument, Jeff swung over the side to clamber nimbly down the rope ladder.

Moments later Rae watched him wade up onto the shore. His clothes pouring seawater, he stooped down to examine the footprints she had spotted. Cautiously, then, he shoved his way through the thick brush screening the crescent of beach from what lay beyond.

Minutes passed. Three, five, seven. At eight, growing increasingly uneasy, Rae had to stifle the impulse to call Jeff's name to make certain he was all right. At ten she finished kicking off her sandals and followed the route he had taken, down the rope ladder and into the warm, salty depths of the Gulf. Sloshing up on the shore, she wished earnestly that she'd had a gun of her own to bring along. Or at least some sturdy boots. His warning about snakes and gators was returning to give her the heebie-jeebies.

But the thought of reptiles wasn't half so scary as the sound of the voice that suddenly came from the other side of a thick stand of mangrove. Rae caught her breath and nearly wavered in her resolve to find out what was going on before steeling herself to press forward once again. Carefully, a leaf at a time, she cleared a little peephole for herself through the layers of foliage, and had to bite her lip to keep from crying out in earnest this time.

Dr. Hamilton lay motionless in the center of a small clearing, his hands and feet bound with twisted cord. Looking distinctly uncomfortable, Manuel Villanova twisted his own hands in agitation, then hauled out a handkerchief to blot his forehead while waiting for his two companions to say something. Jeff waited, too, a defiant look on his face. It was clearly up to Alyssa Fairfax to speak, and she did, spitting out the question she had asked once before.

"I asked you why you brought that girl along! You were supposed to come and collect us here, not go joyriding with your cute little redhead. But I'd forgotten—you've grown to be dear old friends by now, haven't you?"

"I like Rae, yes." A lot better than he liked Alyssa at that moment, Jeff's expression declared. "But I never would have dragged her into this if I hadn't been boxed in. She knew our friend here and the guy on the ground had come out this way to do some shelling. Somehow or other she got the idea into her head that he might need assistance. The people up at the lab are spreading the alarm too. If I had refused to take her, she was going to get one of the deputies to drive her out."

"That would have been just too bad for both of them," Alyssa snapped. "Never mind. We can dispose of her later. There are plenty of sharks—"

"No!" Jeff said belligerently. "Forget it, Alyssa. I agreed to do a little chauffeuring back and forth between here and Alta Monte to keep the *Coral Belle* when the bank was getting ready to foreclose on her, but I draw the line at murdering my friends. It won't take me long to run Rae back to Shell Bay and drop her off at the wharf before coming back to pick up you two. Why don't you let me take the doctor back too? You don't even need him. You already have all the findings from that research they were doing up at the lab."

"That reminds me," Alyssa cut in rudely. "Give it here, Manuel. I want to make absolutely sure that disc stays safe. The way you're always mopping your forehead, that phony head of hair of yours is apt to fly off in midocean."

"You'd sweat, too, if someone made you wear a thing that weighs as much as this does," Villanova protested. "But I did it without complaint, didn't I? Smuggled that disc out nice as you please between those woven layers of insulating material. It's up to your people now to let me and my mother go!"

Shock closed in around Rae like water overwhelming a swimmer going down for the third time. She gripped the tree trunk beside her, clinging to the damp, rough bark heedless of the splinters piercing her skin. It felt almost as if she were drowning in all the revelations she'd overheard.

There seemed to be no doubt that the *Coral Belle* was the vessel Simon had been sent here to locate. The ferryboat. With her own ears she'd heard Jeff admit that he had agreed to cooperate with the extremists on Alta Monte to keep the bank from foreclosing on his cabin cruiser. Just a little while earlier the thought had crossed Rae's mind that Jeff Carter was fonder of his boat than he could ever be of any woman. But that he should put his country second—

It was a jolt, realizing that the *Coral Belle* was the sinister "ferryboat." Especially since yesterday Simon and Norm Peters had headed up to Port Charlotte to check out a boat they'd been eager to locate. But at least Rae no longer needed to wonder how the computer program Alyssa had stolen had been smuggled out of the lab. That very special toupee Manuel Villanova wore provided the perfect cache.

She could sympathize with the unfortunate man. It was all too obvious that he'd been forced to cooperate with the terrorists because of threats to his mother. She could guess now why he'd kept hanging around the communications room at the lab. Somehow he must have hoped to get a call through to the island that had always been his home, to make certain his mother had not been harmed. But even with the pressure he'd been under, his professional conscience had impelled him to write to Dr. Rausch, exposing the whole plot.

Sounds of a scuffle drew Rae's attention back to the clearing. While she'd been putting two and two together and drawing some pretty frightening conclusions, she had missed hearing Alyssa's reply. Whatever she'd said had been enough to make Villanova fly into a rage. Looking as if he were capable of throttling her with his bare hands, he made a lunge at her. Big as he was, it was all Jeff could do to pull him away. Rae had a dreadful feeling that there was no longer any cause to worry about Señora Villanova, that she was now beyond help. Her son had been forced to sacrifice his ideals only to learn that he had been betrayed.

The expression on Alyssa's face as she watched Jeff struggling to restrain Villanova tipped Rae off to something else too. She had the look of Morris eyeing a catnip mouse. No wonder Alyssa had singled her out for some special spite! She was jealous of Rae because of the dates she and Jeff had had. Remembering the man-sized portions of food in that shopping cart, she felt certain that Jeff was the person slated to share that Labor Day cookout with Alyssa—weather permitting or not. No wonder the darned woman had chosen the computer terminal at Rae's workstation to sabotage.

Alyssa hated her. Enough to mention sharks.

The realization hit Rae with the power of a thunderbolt. It wasn't just Dr. Hamilton whose life was in danger. Her own could very well be on the line too. So far Jeff had refused to cooperate with Alyssa's demands, but that could change any time. Rae gulped as she remembered his warning not to go walking into any situation she couldn't handle. Now she knew exactly what he'd been talking about.

A glance over her shoulder showed the *Coral Belle* riding quietly at anchor. Back there in the clearing the oddly matched confederates were still squabbling among themselves. If she hurried, there was an outside chance that she could bring help back in time to rescue Dr. Hamilton and take the others into custody.

Heart pounding, Rae let the leaves fall back into place. Noiselessly, she retraced her steps across the damp sand. She took a last look out at the cruiser as she prepared to plunge into the surf. A flash of rippling color caught her eye. Once, she remembered,

Brian had told her about a highly effective distress signal. By the time she had climbed the rope ladder and swung herself back onto the *Coral Belle's* deck, Rae was hoping that she'd found a way of attracting attention to her plight without having to take the boat all the way back to Shell Bay.

The breeze billowed up, whipping the thick cloth into her face. As she clutched the flag to keep it from being blown out of her hands, Rae thought of the way Alyssa had taunted Manuel Villanova about the wind blowing off the heavy toupee he'd been forced to wear. The recollection of that cruel sarcasm made her more determined than ever to thwart Alyssa's plans.

Her task finally accomplished, Rae streaked toward the bow of the big cruiser. It took only a brief search to locate the lever that operated the anchor hoist. Relief hit her as she heard the whine of machinery winching up the ponderous weight. *Good,* Rae thought. *Good!* Now to locate the key that would activate the *Coral Belle's* powerful twin engines.

There was such an array of gauges and dials on the dash that for a moment or two she could only stare at them in confusion. Then, to her tremendous relief, she spotted the switch she'd been looking for.

She reached for it . . . just as a powerful, deeply tanned hand closed over her wrist!

Swinging around, Rae felt her heart nearly stop. Piercing blue eyes bore into hers. The face confronting her was as set and stern as if it had been carved from a log.

"Going somewhere?" Jeff Carter asked.

Never once in her entire life had Rae Travis ever fainted. It was a temptation to do so now—to just collapse into welcome, black oblivion. But Jeff was nobody's fool. If she keeled over, he might interpret it as an admission of guilt. Whereas, if she could keep him from catching on to what she'd been up to—

"Oh, gosh, you scared the living daylights out of me!" There was all too much truth in her ingenious exclamation. "Jeff, I thought you'd *never* get back! I kept picturing snakes and gators—"

"So you swam ashore to see for yourself."

Rae glanced down at her dripping clothing. Two sets of wet footprints trailed across the deck. She prayed that he wouldn't realize hers had taken a detour to the stern. "Ah—no. Just a little dip to cool off."

He didn't even blink. "Won't work, Rae. I saw your tracks in the sand up there. Must have been a shock, realizing that seashells had absolutely nothing to do with the reason Villanova was ordered to bring your friend out here. You can't say I didn't do my best to steer you off, though. Why didn't you just stay ashore once you learned what was going on? Find a good hiding spot and wait for the rest of us to leave?"

"That probably would have been the smartest thing to do," Rae admitted regretfully. "But I really couldn't just cringe behind a bush while poor Dr. Hamilton was kidnapped."

"It's high principles like that that'll get you into trouble every time." Jeff swore under his breath and glanced at his watch. The gesture reminded Rae of another time she'd watched him do the same thing.

"It was a put-up job, wasn't it?" Her stark eyes told him how disappointed she was to learn the truth about his activities. "I mean, finding Manuel Villanova the day we went out fishing. You knew exactly where that rowboat would be found and who'd be in it. All you had to do was wait until the appointed moment, then toss something into the water to rile up the sharks while Dr. Hamilton and I were intent on that tarpon I'd hooked. Their behavior gave you the perfect excuse to start scanning the water for whatever else might be seen. Was there some kind of homing device in the rowboat to bring you right up to it? Was that the real reason you didn't haul it in along with your dinghy?"

"See if I ever get involved with another bright lady." Jeff gave an awkward shrug. "Yeah, Rae. You've got it all figured out. The minute Alyssa heard I was taking the two of you fishing for the old guy's birthday, she saw the opportunity to bring in an accomplice and foist him off on the lab. Villanova and Hamilton had met before, so there was no problem about identification. It was easy enough to radio Alta Monte and get the ball rolling, have her contacts there start planting items in some of the West Indies newspapers—"

"You!" Rae exclaimed. "You were the two shooting at Brian and me in the swamp that night!"

"You'd shoot too if someone suddenly crept up on you in a place like that," Jeff retorted defensively.

"No one got hurt, did they? I put that last shell a good three inches over your brother's head. All I really wanted to do was scare you off."

And instead they had called in the Border Patrol. Rae wondered if that shortwave set would ever show up again. Probably not. Forgetting for a minute that Jeff wasn't the friend she'd always considered him, she looked up at him, eyes wide. "Who is she, really? That woman over there who calls herself Alyssa?"

"What do you think I am, Interpol? She's a zealot from one of those Middle Eastern countries where it's against the law to drink or smoke but okay to chop people's heads off." Jeff shook his own head, looking as if he regretted ever having become entangled with the group from the Enclave. "On a run I made a few months back, one of her cohorts let slip a few home truths about her. She's an expert at disguises. This isn't the first time she spotted a tourist whose face resembled her own closely enough for her to pull off an ambitious impersonation."

Rae bit her lip. "The real Alyssa Fairfax—"

"Disappeared somewhere in Greece, the way I heard it told. She won't be coming back." Jeff glanced toward shore. "And neither will you, Rae. Not if she has anything to say about it. I'm sorry. I never pictured it ending like this between us."

She opened her mouth to protest, but when she saw the gun come out of its waterproof pouch, Rae knew they were past the point of arguments. Past the point of no return. As the heavy butt of the pistol swung toward her skull, her last thought was that she would never see Simon again.

Chapter Eleven

Four days later, Rae found herself gazing at the most beautiful sight in the world—Simon's profile. They were in the front seat of his green sedan, and he was driving her to work.

"How's the sunburn today?" he asked.

She gave him a rueful smile. Though he had paused at a stoplight, she had no inclination whatsoever to twist the rearview mirror around for a quick look. She knew, worse luck, what the glass would reveal.

"As you can no doubt tell, it's reached the itchy, peeling stage," she replied. "But, oh, Simon, I was so fortunate! A blistered nose and a bit of a concussion are minor irritations compared to the fate I'd have met if Alyssa had had her way. I only hope the courts take that into consideration before handing down Jeff's sentence."

"I suspect that they will. He still has an awful lot to answer for, though."

Simon wasn't having an easy time sorting out his feelings toward Jeff. He felt sure Jeff had been more than a little in love with Rae, a sentiment with which he could readily identify. Whether out of love, friendship, or a determination to steer clear of murder, Jeff had more than likely saved her life. After knocking her unconscious, he had towed her ashore, then stashed her inert body out of sight. Then, according to the testimony of Cole Hamilton, he'd boldly returned to the clearing and insisted that Rae had escaped.

Turning onto the main highway, Simon drove steadily in the direction of the Avionics Lab. On the other hand, he went on ruminating, Jeff Carter and his "ferryboat," the *Coral Belle,* had been running rings around the authorities for a long time. A smuggling charge was likely to be the least of what Jeff would be facing. And it wasn't until the very end, when Simon and Norm had made a quick trip up to Port Charlotte to check over a rowboat washed ashore during the storm, that the truth had dawned on Simon. That cleverly concealed homing device affixed to the little craft Manuel Villanova had used for his "escape" had tipped him off to the fact that Jeff was the man they'd been looking for all along.

This was Wednesday, Rae's first day back at work after the ordeal of being knocked out and stranded on a deserted beach for several endless hours. Concussions had been known to cause people to see double and suffer dizzy spells. Just to be on the safe side, Simon had volunteered to drive Rae back and forth to the lab for the rest of the week.

He pulled to a stop in front of the heavily guarded gate. "Don't let 'em work you too hard, okay?"

"Okay." Rae unfastened her seat belt and clung to his hand for a moment, letting him know she appreciated the special treatment. "See you at four?"

"I won't be late. We're overdue for a long, serious talk."

They certainly were, Rae silently agreed. After climbing out, she stood still for a moment, watching the car pull away. She seemed to be doing that a lot lately. Unfortunately, it was probably a mere preview of things to come. Between Hurricane Jonathan and the mind-boggling events following the storm, there had been no chance at all for the two of them to discuss their future. With a pang of distress she realized that Simon's assignment here in Shell Bay must be all but wrapped up.

They'd work it out, she told herself resolutely as she pinned on her ID badge and turned toward the gate. They would. Somehow. Simon had told her so, and she had great faith in him. In the meantime there was a job to be done here. A mighty important job. One that she had deliberately muffed a few days earlier.

By noon each member of the team had finished entering the correct data to bring phase one of Project G.A.T.E. to completion. Rae looked down at the computer keyboard in surprise as she added her name to the end of the guardian-angel package she'd just finished programming. She realized that she'd been subconsciously waiting for the darned thing to break down.

"Why the grin?" Cole Hamilton asked, entering

her office as she called a "Come in" over her shoulder.

Rae switched off the machine in relief. "It just dawned on me that Alyssa really was an inspired computer technician. She could play this complicated gizmo like Itzhak Perlman plays his Stradivarius, even to the point of engineering it to break down exactly on schedule. Think we're going to miss her around here?"

There was no need for Dr. Hamilton to fake a shudder. "Most people would agree with me that the world is well rid of that one. I doubt we will ever know her true identity, but the woman was a complete fanatic. She actually intended to try shooting it out with that Coast Guard cutter that hailed us a few miles from shore. Her finger was curled around the trigger when Manuel Villanova darted across the deck to tackle her."

What had happened after that was a confused melee, by all accounts. All Rae knew for sure was that in the struggle between the terrorist and her Latino victim, the woman masquerading as Alyssa Fairfax had been knocked overboard. The *Coral Belle*'s propellers had spared her a trial and a lifetime in prison.

"Whether he meant to or not, Señor Villanova certainly got his revenge!"

Rae's suspicion as she witnessed that angry scene in the clearing on Saturday morning had since been confirmed. The elderly woman had succumbed to her illness within days of her son's enforced voyage on that rowboat. Manuel Villanova had always hated the terrorists, but hearing Alyssa taunt him with the news of his mother's demise had goaded him into an avenging rage.

Dr. Hamilton furnished a bit of information that hadn't as yet been made public. "Thanks to Manuel's accounts of conditions on his island, there's a campaign underway to oust the groups from the Enclave—from the Western Hemisphere altogether. Villanova is spearheading a resolution to be brought up before the United Nations. It calls not only for the foreign extremists to be deported, but for a more responsible government to be installed there under the administration of the OAS."

"Good!" Rae welcomed the news that not only her own country but the Organization of American States was stepping in at last. "Felipe Muñoz isn't fit to dictate terms to an anthill. I hope he's exiled to someplace like Devil's Island for throwing Alta Monte open to the terrorists."

Terrorists like Alyssa. Or . . . not Alyssa. "I wish we knew who she really was," Rae added pensively. "It's outrageous that some poor dead girl from Charleston should continue to have her name reviled. My . . . a friend of mine secured a copy of the real Alyssa's college yearbook. There was quite a strong superficial resemblance, but no one who'd been personally acquainted with her would have been deceived as to which person was which."

"No doubt that's the main reason that the woman who almost torpedoed Project G.A.T.E. didn't dare return to Charleston to do a little in-depth work on her South Carolina accent." Cole Hamilton shook his head. "She really was a clever mimic of languages and voices."

"Not clever enough to fool my dad," Rae proclaimed. "He knew the minute he heard her speak that she hadn't been born in this country."

"That's what did it?" Dr. Hamilton asked wonderingly. "You took the risks you did on the strength of five minutes' conversation in a grocery store?"

"Well, it was my father's insistence that brought matters to a head, but there were lots of other little pointers too. All of them much more closely based on instinct than science, and not a shred of proof in the lot. I knew that a fair-minded man like Emil Rausch would never have considered postponing wrapping up the program on the basis of a mere hunch."

"But now that you've proved your case, I can assure you that some internal features were added to our computer system to make it impossible to duplicate anything being programmed into its memory banks. This experience taught the Security people a grave lesson. And demonstrated what a high potential value the work we are doing here must have."

The scientist lapsed into silence. Rae felt sure that he was thinking of the family he had lost aboard an airliner which hadn't been equipped with the newly designed safeguards included in Project G.A.T.E.

"Come on," she urged, taking his arm. "Let's go down to the cafeteria and have something to eat. At home my dad's been going heavy on invalid food like chicken soup and oatmeal ever since Saturday. To tell the truth, I'm ready for a good old-fashioned plate of spaghetti and meatballs."

Rae was not destined to eat her lunch in peace, however. Again and again friends and acquaintances stopped by the table with awestruck questions.

"Is it true that you turned the flag upside down on that cabin cruiser?" the receptionist asked.

"Yes, it sounds like a terrible thing to do, but years ago my brother, who's in the Coast Guard, told me about a ship in trouble using that particular distress signal," Rae replied. "Brian said it was a highly effective SOS. That's the way it turned out this time, thank heaven. The crew of a cutter on patrol spotted the inverted flag and immediately hailed the *Coral Belle.*"

"It's amazing that the passengers aboard the boat didn't see it themselves," somebody else exclaimed.

"Having been a hostage aboard the cruiser that day, I can assure you that they had other things on their minds," Dr. Hamilton said, tactfully neglecting to add that the flaming argument between the charter-boat captain and the female terrorist had centered around Rae Travis. Alyssa—whatever her real name was—had been furious that Rae had managed to escape. Again and again she'd accused Jeff Carter of having a hand in the matter. The last thing either of them had been paying heed to that morning was whether the Stars and Stripes was flying upright in its usual position.

* * *

Simon was waiting when Rae came through the gate that afternoon. He came forward to meet her and slid a supportive arm across her shoulders. "You look tired."

"I am." She brushed back a lock of hair drooping across her forehead. "There was lots of work to catch up on, and of course at lunch everybody had a million questions to ask."

"So you wound up answering them instead of cleaning up your plate. We'll take care of that first thing," Simon assured her. "How about a nice hot bowl of chicken soup?"

"How about a nice gooey pizza," Rae countered, "with everything on it except the anchovies?"

He had to laugh at her yearning tone. "Sounds like the way to my woman's heart is through her stomach."

"Well, I wouldn't say that was the only route, but I wouldn't call it a detour, either," Rae said with a laugh.

After using the phone in the pizza parlor to let her dad know that she wouldn't be home until later, she rejoined Simon. Rae had had no intention of raising any serious questions so soon. But looking at the man she adored, she found herself unable to bear the suspense of not knowing how much time they had left to spend together.

"Simon, have—have you got your new assignment yet?"

"Uh-huh." Reaching across the table, he caught hold of her left hand. "It came through today."

She swallowed hard, pushing down the lump in her throat. "I see. Well, it's good to know they don't waste any time in the Border Patrol."

"One of the few things that slows us down is hurricanes." He had been concealing a small object in his palm. Now Simon guided the dainty circlet onto her finger. "I'd have given this to you sooner if it hadn't been for Jonathan."

Misty-eyed, Rae gazed down at the beautiful star sapphire. "Simon, it's—"

"An engagement ring," he supplied helpfully.

"But how—when—are you sure?" Her words tumbled out awkwardly. "How are we going to—"

"You're one for questions, aren't you? But how about an answer first?"

"Simon, I'd give anything in the world to marry you, you must know that."

"I'll take that as a yes. Good. Then it's all settled."

"But—"

Simon continued as if she hadn't said anything. "I've already spoken with your father. He seems to think I'll make an adequate son-in-law. Particularly since I don't intend to take you very far away."

Rae looked from him to the ring, then back again. "You . . . don't?"

"Get that stiff expression off your face, sweetheart. I have no intention of going off to Nogales or anyplace else without you." Simon brought her fingertips to his lips. "I've had seven good years in the Border

Patrol. Time to let someone else take my place on the enforcement end of things. I requested an intra-agency transfer, into the regular Immigration service. It's a better kind of job for a married man who wants to spend evenings and weekends with his family. Best of all, there's a full-time opening up at the Naples office."

"Naples, Florida?" Rae's eyes shone with joyful hope.

"Did you think I meant Naples, Italy? Yes, sweetheart. Naples, Florida," Simon assured her. "Just a few miles up the coast. I figured we might look around for a house halfway between there and Shell Bay. Make an easy commute for both of us."

Rae brought their linked hands back to her side of the table, pressing his to her cheek. "That's the best idea I've heard in ages."

"Wait." Simon's dark eyes were filled with promise. "Just wait, my love. The best is yet to come."